She  ~~thought about moving~~ ser and, um, ~~...~~ could be awk~~...~~

If he ~~...~~ didn't do casua~~...~~ f Desmond had been secretly pining for her.

It had been over a decade since their prom date. If he'd been so interested, he could have easily asked her out a thousand different times. But he hadn't. So making a move would be stupid. He would be way too nice in his refusal and she would feel like an idiot.

And just like that, whatever vague fantasy she'd been harboring disappeared with a nearly audible poof.

"All right, then," she said with a forced smile. "Good night."

She closed her door behind her, then leaned against it.

No more Desmond-is-handsome-and-sexy thoughts, she told herself. She was going to live here for two months and she needed to remember that and act like a polite but disinterested roommate. Anything else was a slick, steep road to disaster, and no one wanted that.

Dear Reader,

For many happy years, Special Edition was my writing home, and I'm thrilled to be back with a story I know will fill your heart. *Before Summer Ends* started life last year as an Audible exclusive. When Special Edition asked if they could make it available to their readers in print and ebook, I jumped at the chance because I knew many of you would want this heartwarming romance for your keeper shelf.

Nissa is the kind of plucky woman I admire. She has a dream, and she'll do anything to achieve it. She'll work a series of side hustles during her summer vacation from teaching. She'll rent out her condo for the extra cash. She'll even move in with her secret crush, Desmond Stilling, her brother's billionaire best friend. I think you'll fall in love with Nissa and Desmond as they fall for each other.

Happy reading,

Susan Mallery

Before Summer Ends

SUSAN MALLERY

SPECIAL EDITION™

Recycling programs
for this product may
not exist in your area.

ISBN-13: 978-1-335-40482-4

Before Summer Ends

This edition published by arrangement with Harlequin Books S.A.

For questions and comments about the quality of this book, please contact us at CustomerService@Harlequin.com.

Harlequin Enterprises ULC
22 Adelaide St. West, 40th Floor
Toronto, Ontario M5H 4E3, Canada
www.Harlequin.com

Printed in U.S.A.

Susan Mallery is the #1 *New York Times* bestselling author of novels about the relationships that define women's lives—family, friendship and romance. *Library Journal* says, "Mallery is the master of blending emotionally believable characters in realistic situations," and readers seem to agree—forty million copies of her books have been sold worldwide. Her warm, humorous stories make the world a happier place to live.

Susan grew up in California and now lives in Seattle with her husband. She's passionate about animal welfare, especially that of the two Ragdoll cats and adorable poodle who think of her as Mom. Visit Susan online at www.susanmallery.com.

Books by Susan Mallery

The Vineyard at Painted Moon
The Friendship List
The Summer of Sunshine & Margot
California Girls
When We Found Home
Secrets of the Tulip Sisters
Daughters of the Bride

Mischief Bay

Sisters Like Us
A Million Little Things
The Friends We Keep
The Girls of Mischief Bay

For a complete list of titles available from Susan Mallery, please visit www.susanmallery.com.

For Nissa—thanks for lending me your name

Chapter One

NISSA

"Darling, we're pregnant!"

"We are?" Nissa Lang asked, somewhat confused by the "we," as well as the news of the pregnancy.

Mimi was in her midforties and as far as Nissa knew, Mimi and her husband hadn't even been trying. Not that Nissa could be sure about that. Her relationship with Mimi was casual at best. Nissa was going to house-sit Mimi's grand mansion while the happy couple spent the summer in a different mansion in Norway. Not only would Nissa get paid a princely sum for things like flushing the many toilets and making sure the gardeners (yes, plural) did their thing, the money was going directly into her I'm-turning-thirty-and-to-prove-my-life-isn't-a-disaster, I'm-taking-myself-to-Italy-for-three-weeks-next-summer fund.

Knowing she had a place to live for July and August, Nissa had rented out her own small condo, to add even more money to her fund. Only the sinking feeling in her stomach told her that maybe she was about to get some bad news in that department.

Mimi laughed. "I know it's a shock. We're stunned. We didn't think we were ever going to be able to have children, but I'm pregnant and it's wonderful. I'm calling because the baby means a change in plans. Between my age and the previous miscarriages, I'm a high-risk pregnancy, and travel is out of the question. So we'll be staying home this summer. I hope you understand."

Yup, there it was. Disappointment on a stick, stabbing her right in her travel dreams.

"Of course," Nissa said politely, because that was how she'd been raised, but on the inside, she was pouting and stomping her feet. "Congratulations. You must be thrilled."

"Thank you. We're beyond happy. Take care. Bye."

With that, Mimi hung up and Nissa sank onto the sofa. She looked at the open boxes scattered around her small condo, the ones she was filling up with personal items so the charming young couple who had rented her place for two months would have room for their own things. She glanced at the calendar she'd tacked on the wall, with the date she was supposed to be out circled in red.

"This is bad," she breathed, letting the phone drop onto the cushion next to her. "What am I going to do?"

She didn't have a summer job lined up, the way she usually did. As a fourth-grade teacher, she had summers off and used the time to get a job to supplement her income. It was how she'd managed to scrape together the down payment for her small condo. She'd moved in nearly a year ago and loved every inch of the place.

She was going to use the Mimi house-sitting money and the rental income for her condo to pay for her Italy trip next year. Postponing it was not an option. Two years ago she and her fiancé of three years had broken up. Before that, her best friend had been diagnosed with kidney disease—the kind that would kill her if she didn't eventually get a transplant. Nissa had firsthand knowledge that life didn't always turn out how you expected or wanted, so putting things off was taking a serious chance of losing out. Something she wasn't willing to risk.

She'd been dreaming about going to Italy since she was fourteen years old. She'd devoured guidebooks, watched travel videos on YouTube and had planned and replanned her stay. Next year, she was spending her thirtieth birthday in Italy.

The problem was, she'd just lost her funding.

Oh, she was putting aside a little every month, but living in the Seattle area was expensive and it wasn't as if she had a six-figure salary. The summer money was how she was going to make the trip happen.

She leaned back against the cushions and considered her options. Obviously, she would have to get a different job. It was already late June, so she might not have a lot of options, what with competing with high school and college students for the best ones. Regardless, she would find something. The more pressing problem was where she was going to live for the next two months.

Her parents would happily welcome her for the summer, but they lived in a small town in Eastern Washington. There wouldn't be many job opportunities if she stayed with them. Plus Nissa didn't want to be that far away from Marisol and her kids. Not when a transplant could show up at any time.

Crashing at Marisol's place wasn't going to work. While her best friend would welcome her, the house was tiny and already overcrowded. Which left one option.

She grabbed her phone and scrolled through her contacts. Shane picked up on the second ring.

"Hey, kid."

She smiled. "You think you're such a big brother, don't you?"

"It's kind of my thing."

"I'm surprised I caught you. Why aren't you slicing and dicing?"

"I just got out of surgery. Knee replacement. The patient is going to be very happy with the outcome."

Shane was an orthopedic surgeon in a busy sports medicine practice. Four years older and definitely the smarter of the two children in the family, he'd always been driven to be the best. Nissa knew she was much more in the "average" category and was comfortable there. She didn't need to change the world, just improve her small part of it.

"I'm glad for your patient," she said. "I need to come live with you for the next two months. And don't you dare say no. You have that extra bedroom. I know you do—I helped you decorate it."

She explained how her house-sitting job had fallen through.

"I'd love to help, but I can't." Shane's voice dropped nearly an octave. "I've met someone."

She resisted rolling her eyes, mostly because he couldn't see her doing it. "Shane, I refuse to accept that as an excuse. You've always met someone. You spend your life 'meeting someone.' It's the sticking with them for longer than three weeks that doesn't work for you."

"This is different. No can do, kid. I can't have you hanging around when I'm trying to...you know."

"Seduce a perfectly nice woman who doesn't know you're going to be a hit-and-run lover? While that sounds great, I'm in trouble. It's serious and I need your help. I have people showing up in three days to move into my place. I need somewhere to go."

"Stay with Desmond."

"What?" she asked, her voice more of a yelp than she would have liked. "No. I can't."

What a ridiculous suggestion. Desmond? As if.

"He has a giant house and he's practically family."

The key word being *practically*. He was, in fact, her brother's best friend from boarding school. Because Shane had gotten a scholarship to the fancy place when he'd been thirteen, and he and Desmond had been close ever since.

Desmond was great. Nissa liked him just fine. He'd taken her to her senior prom when her boyfriend had dumped her at the last minute. She'd warned him not to marry his now ex-wife and she'd been right.

"It's a perfect solution," Shane said cheerfully. "I'm going to text him right now."

"What? No. You can't. I'm not—"

The rapid *beep, beep, beep* told her she was talking to herself. Shane had already hung up.

"I'm not comfortable staying with him," she muttered to no one in particular.

Not that she could explain exactly why to her brother. Or herself. In truth, the thought of living with Desmond made her insides get all twisty. It would be too strange.

Besides, what were the odds of him agreeing? He wouldn't. Why would he? People didn't generally enjoy having unannounced roommates for months on end. He would say no. She was sure of it. Practically sure. Mostly sure.

For the second time in less than ten minutes, she dropped her phone onto the sofa cushion and knew she was totally and completely screwed.

DESMOND

Stilling Holdings, Inc., or SHI as everyone called the company, was a multinational conglomerate with interests in everything from rare element mining to biofuels to construction to infrastructure. The different divisions were managed as separate companies, each division president reporting directly to CEO Desmond Stilling.

Three years ago, Desmond had moved the company headquarters from San Francisco to just north of Seattle. A new ten-story building had been constructed, SHI had adopted six elementary schools, two middle schools and a high school as their local charity projects, and on most days Desmond managed to stay on top of everything work related. Every now and then circumstances bested him. An airport strike in South America had delayed shipment of needed parts to a plant in Germany, leaving road crews in Eastern Europe without crucial equipment. Every day of delay was a problem in a part of the world where there was a season for construction.

In the end, he'd had his people charter two planes out of a private airfield forty kilometers away. By Tuesday of next week, the completed machinery would be on its way and the road work could continue. The cost of the chartered planes would chew up any profit, but he knew the road was more important. He would make up the money elsewhere. He always did.

Shortly after eleven, his personal cell phone buzzed. He pulled it out and smiled when he saw the name and picture displayed.

"No, I can't take off the rest of the day and go hiking with you," he said by way of greeting. "Some of us have to work for a living."

"I work," Shane protested with a laugh. "I save lives, my friend."

"You replace joints, not hearts."

"I improve quality of life. What do you do?"

"I build roads and feed the world. This is me, winning."

The familiar banter was a welcome relief from the fast-paced, business-only rhythm of his day. Much to the chagrin of his staff, Desmond got to the office early and stayed late. When he'd been married, he'd had something to go home to, but these days, there wasn't much waiting for him in his big house, so he stayed at work later and later.

He knew he would have to make a change at some point—just not today.

"You think you're such a powerful CEO," Shane said.

"I *am* a powerful CEO."

"You're talking but all I hear is a buzzing sound." Shane chuckled. "Okay, enough of that. I need a favor."

"Done."

"You don't know what I want."

Desmond knew it didn't matter. Shane was his best friend and he would do anything for him or a member of his family. Desmond had grown up the classically clichéd lonely, rich child. The first ten years of his life, he'd been homeschooled with excellent tutors. When he'd finally been sent off to boarding school, he'd had the education of a college freshman but the social skills of a pencil. The transition had been difficult.

Two years later, he'd been sent to a college prep school where Shane had been his roommate. They'd quickly become friends. That first Christmas, Shane had dragged him home for the holiday. Inside his friend's modest house, Desmond had experienced what a family was supposed to be. For the first time in his life, he'd seen parents hugging their children and had felt warmth and affection. The presents had been chosen with care and love rather than ordered by staff. For those two weeks, he'd been just like everyone else and it had been glorious.

Ever since then, the Langs had been a part of his life. He would do anything for any of them, regardless of what they needed. His parents were still alive, but the Langs were his real family.

"Nissa needs a place to stay for a couple of months. She had a gig house-sitting but that fell through. She's rented out her condo. I'm guessing backing out on that contract could be a problem. Plus she wants the money for her trip to Italy next summer."

Technically Nissa wanted to go to Rome and Florence, rather than generically visit Italy, but Desmond didn't correct his friend. Nor did he mention he was the one who had introduced Nissa to Mimi and her husband when Mimi had said they were looking for a dependable house sitter. Of course Mimi's unexpected pregnancy would have changed their plans. He should have realized that himself.

"She can stay with me," he said. "There's plenty of room."

"That's what I said. You have what? Twelve bedrooms?"

"Eight."

At least he thought there were eight. Maybe it was ten. After his initial tour of the house before he'd bought it, he'd never much gone exploring. He used his bedroom, his home office and the media room. The rest of the house didn't interest him.

"So that's a yes?" Shane asked.

"It is. I'll get in touch with her today and find out when she wants to move in, then I'll let my housekeeper know and she'll get a room put together."

"Thanks, bro. I appreciate it. You're doing us both a big favor. So let's go out on your boat sometime soon."

"I'd like that."

"I'm on call for the next two weekends, but after that."

"Let me know what days work for you. We'll have fun."

"Thanks for helping with Nissa."

"Anytime."

They talked for a few more minutes, then hung up. Desmond glanced at his computer. But instead of rows of numbers, he saw Nissa in her prom dress, earnestly thanking him for offering to take her to the dance at her high school. He'd been in the first year of his MBA program then, having finished his undergraduate degree in three years. He'd flown up from Stanford to be her date.

At the time, he'd been doing a favor for a friend, but the second he saw her, everything changed. Gone was the preteen who had tagged along whenever he'd visited. In her place was a beautiful woman with big eyes and a mouth he couldn't stop staring at, and later kissing.

But nothing more. No matter how much he'd wanted to take things to the next level, he'd known he couldn't. She was the only daughter of his surrogate family. He loved and respected the Langs too much to betray their trust in him. So he'd done the right thing and had firmly put Nissa in the friend column, where she had stayed. And would stay.

He shook off the memories and quickly sent a text.

Shane says you need a place to stay. I have plenty of room. Just tell me when you want to be there and I'll get a room ready.

There was a pause, then he saw three dots, followed by her reply.

Really? You will? I seriously doubt you know where the spare sheets are kept.

He chuckled. You're right, but I'll have it done. Hilde will be thrilled to have someone else to care for. I disappoint her with my boring lifestyle.

Desmond, you're nice to offer, but I couldn't possibly impose.

I insist. There's plenty of room. **He hesitated, then added,** It's not your parents' house. Whoever you're seeing is welcome to stay over.

As in a boy? LOL That part of my life is a disaster. Kind of like yours. Can I LOL twice in a text without seeming like I'm getting weird?

You can if you'd like. When do you want to move in?

Gulp. Is Friday too soon?

It's not. I'll let Hilde know. Text me when you have an approximate time so I can make sure I'm home to give you a tour and a key.

Thanks, Desmond. You're the best. I promise to be the perfect guest. You won't even know I'm there.

He studied her words, thinking that he very much wanted to know she was there. He would have offered his place, regardless, but he'd always liked Nissa. She was easy to be around, and he felt comfortable in her presence. With her, he didn't feel as much the heartless bastard the women he dated always ended up claiming he was. Plus she'd been right about Rosemary and he'd been the fool who hadn't listened.

See you Friday, he texted.

Thanks again.

He sent a quick text to Hilde, telling her about Nissa's stay. When his housekeeper sent back questions about the types of foods Nissa liked and which bedroom would be best, he gave Hilde Nissa's number so the two of them could work it out. Once that was done, he returned his attention to his computer, because work was the one place where he had all the answers.

NISSA

Friday morning Nissa got up early to finish getting ready for her move-out. She'd packed her personal things, along with a few breakables she didn't want to leave out. All that was left was her grandmother's china and her clothes. She would take care of the clothes first thing, then wait for Shane to arrive to help her with the china. Once that was done, she would give her place a final clean, then head over to Desmond's house.

So far she'd done a good job of ignoring her upcoming living situation. If she didn't think about moving into the big house on the Sound and, you know, living with *him*, she didn't get nervous. But if she allowed herself to dwell on the reality of sharing a roof with a guy she'd had a crush on for over a decade, she got a little queasy.

Not that her crush meant anything, she reminded herself as she got dressed before heading for the bathroom. It was just a funny quirk, left over from when she'd been a teenager. Desmond had been older, fantastically good-looking and sweet to her. Of course she'd liked him. Now, as a grown-up, she knew those feelings were just remnants of happy memories. These days they were friends. Good friends. He'd been married, for heaven's sake, and she'd been engaged. They'd both moved on. Or at least she had—she doubted he had anything to move on from. So there was nothing to worry about or any reason to be nervous. Really.

That somewhat decided, she finished getting ready, then put together several boxes and got out packing paper. She set everything on her dining room table. Shortly after eight, her doorbell rang.

She let in her brother, smiling when she saw the to-go tray he carried.

"Morning," he said, giving her a quick kiss on the cheek. "I brought breakfast."

"I see that. Thank you."

She took the coffee and breakfast sandwich he offered, then led the way to the sofa in her living room. They set their food on the coffee table. Shane glanced around at the bare side tables and nearly empty floating shelves.

"You were robbed."

She sipped her coffee before smiling at him. "You know how I am. I have stuff everywhere. No one wants to live with that. So I put it all away. It's very clean looking, don't you think?"

"I don't know. It makes me feel as if you've been taken over by aliens." He nodded at the small hutch in the dining alcove. "We're just wrapping up the china?"

She nodded. "It's a full set for twelve. I don't want anything to get broken. I made space in my storage unit, so we can take the boxes down there."

"Sounds like a plan. You're moving in with Desmond after that?"

"This afternoon." She wanted to protest that she wasn't moving in with him—not in the traditional sense. But saying that would cause her brother to start asking questions and there was no way she wanted to explain about her crush-slash-fluttery stomach.

"So what's with the new girlfriend?" she asked, hoping to distract him. "Who is she and what makes her 'the one'?" She made air quotes with her free hand.

"Her name is Coreen and she's an ER pediatrician."

"A doctor," she teased. "Mom and Dad will be so proud."

He grinned. "I know. I'm the favorite for a reason, kid."

"Oh, please. They so love me more."

The joking was familiar. Shane might be more brilliant but she was no less adored by her parents. They hadn't had a lot of money for fancy things when she'd been growing up but there had been plenty of attention and affection.

"You didn't answer my question," she pointed out as she picked up her breakfast sandwich. "Why is she special?"

"I don't know. She's smart and pretty and I like her a lot." He took a bite of his sandwich. "There's something about her. We'll see how it goes. I'm optimistic and I don't want to mess up anything."

"Why would you think you mess up your relationships?"

"I'm not like you," he said. "I've never made being in love work."

That surprised her. "Not with any of the women you've dated?"

He shook his head. "There's always an issue." One corner of his mouth turned up. "Unlike you and Desmond." He made kissing noises. "You've always had a thing for him."

She willed herself not to blush, then socked him in the arm. "I had a crush on him when I was a kid. So what?"

"You followed him around like a puppy."

"He was dreamy."

Shane scowled. "Please don't say dreamy before I've finished my breakfast."

"Deal with it, brother of mine. So when do I get to meet the magical Coreen?"

"Not for a while. I want to make sure it lasts. What about you? Who's the new guy?"

"There is no new guy." Her love life was sadly lacking.

"You haven't been involved since you broke up with James. Come on, Nissa. That's been what? Two years? It's time to move on."

"I know and I want to. But it's hard to meet people. My luck with online dating is nonexistent and all the guys I meet through work are married."

"There have to be a few single dads with kids in your class."

She looked at him pityingly. "I don't date students' fathers. It's tacky and against policy."

"That makes sense. What about when you go to Italy? You can meet someone there. A handsome Italian with a nice accent."

She laughed. "Technically if we're in Italy, I'll be the one with the accent." She was less sure about a vacation romance. Not that she would object to being swept off her feet for a week or two but she doubted the affair would last past her time there.

"Want me to ask around at my practice? See if any of my work friends know of a single guy."

"No. Absolutely not. I shudder at the thought." The last thing she needed was her brother finding her guys to date.

"Hey, I have good taste."

"You've never set me up, so we don't actually know that." She tempered her words with a smile. "But thank you for thinking about me."

"I always think about you. You're my baby sister and I want you to be happy." He grinned. "And safe. Why else would I have told Desmond to walk away after your prom date?"

She'd been about to take the last bite of her sandwich. Instead she stared at her brother, her mouth hanging open.

"What?" she managed, trying to make sense of his words.

Shane winked. "I know. You're impressed, right? Like I said, I look after you."

She put down the sandwich. "Wait a second. Are you saying Desmond wanted to go out with me after prom?"

"Sure. He had a great time and was all into you, but I pointed out that he was too old and too experienced. He was in grad school and you were a senior in high school. No way that was happening on my watch."

The adult side of her brain could appreciate what her brother had done. He was right about both the age and experience difference between them. But the teenaged girl that would be with her always nearly shrieked in protest. She'd liked Desmond—she'd liked him a lot. When he'd disappeared after their one date, she'd been devastated.

"Besides," Shane added, obviously unaware of what she was thinking, "he's a part of the family. I reminded him that he owed my folks for taking him in and stuff, and he shouldn't repay them by going after you."

"You're pretty proud of yourself, aren't you?" she asked, reaching for her coffee.

"I am and you should thank me."

She held in a sigh. He'd done what he thought was right, and at the time, it had been. Her broken heart was her own business. But the information did leave her with some interesting questions, such as if he'd liked her, why hadn't he tried dating her later, when she'd been all grown up? And most important of all—what did he think of her now?

Chapter Two

DESMOND

Desmond had brought home work but couldn't seem to focus on it. Normally he enjoyed getting lost in whatever business project he was involved in. Even the things that most people considered boring—reading contracts or reviewing financial statements—were pleasurable for him. The business was rational—at any given moment he knew exactly where things were and how to improve them. He might not like the answers he came up with, but he knew he could count on them. His business was a place where he excelled. Relationships, particularly the romantic kind, had never been one of his strengths.

Oh, he could get a woman into his bed in a couple of hours. Sex was easy, but anything involving the heart was nearly impossible for him. Probably because he was too much like his parents, he thought, admitting defeat and closing his spreadsheet program. They had raised him to use his head and ignore his emotions, telling him that feelings weren't to be trusted and caring too much made a person weak. They'd certainly demonstrated their philosophy time and time again with him and with each other. There had been no hugs in his family, no displays of affection. Being told he'd done well at something was about as personal as it got when he'd been growing up.

Given the choice between reaching out and holding back, he learned to always hold back. It was what he knew and it was safer. The only place he was different was with Shane and his family. They were the people he trusted.

He remembered when his marriage had ended. Rosemary, who it turned out, hadn't married for much more than a lifestyle, had told him he was the coldest and most heartless man she'd ever known. When he'd protested that he'd been a good and kind husband, she'd laughed at him, telling him he had a chunk of ice in the space where his heart should be.

The end of his marriage had been disappointing—not so much because he missed her but because he didn't. He was supposed to have wanted to spend the rest of his life with her. Shouldn't he have mourned the loss? The fact that he hadn't reinforced her supposition. He was a man without a heart.

He tried to shake off those thoughts and return his attention to his work, but quickly realized that wasn't happening. He obviously wasn't going to get anything done until Nissa arrived and got settled. For some reason, he was more focused on that than the Asian sales report.

He got up and crossed to the large window in his study. The late-June days were long and sunny, and the garden flourished. The grass was dark green, flowers provided plenty of color in the planting beds, the trees looked healthy. The gardeners did a good job, regardless of the seasons, but in the summer, their hard work paid off.

He turned at the sound of the vacuum cleaner being turned on somewhere upstairs. Hilde had been in a state since he'd told her Nissa was coming to stay. There had been cleaning and washing and other tasks he couldn't begin to imagine. The refrigerator overflowed with food and there were fresh flowers everywhere in the house.

Her burst of happy activity made him feel guilty. His housekeeper obviously didn't have enough to do in a day. The house was large, but there wasn't anyone to make a mess. He rarely ate dinner at home, so she wasn't spending much time cooking. He would guess she was bored working for him—a problem he didn't know how to solve. If he'd stayed married to Rosemary, they would have had kids by now. That would have increased the workload. Of course if they'd stayed together, he and Rosemary would have been living in different wings of the house, barely seeing each other, except when they passed in the hallway.

His phone buzzed. He pulled it out, then smiled when he read the text.

I'm here. Just giving you a heads-up because the house is so big, I thought you'd need an extra minute or five to walk to the door and I really don't want to be kept waiting.

He was still chuckling when he heard the doorbell ring a few seconds later.

He walked through the entryway and pulled open the large front door. Nissa stood on the wide, covered porch, her long red hair pulled back in a ponytail. She had on cropped jeans and a T-shirt. Her lack of makeup meant he could see all her freckles—the freckles he'd always liked and that she claimed to hate every time they were mentioned. Her big blue eyes crinkled as she smiled at him.

"Are you out of breath from the long trek? Should I pause until you're able to speak?"

"I can manage a sentence or two," he said as he held open his arms.

She stepped into his embrace easily, as she always had. He hugged her, telling himself not to notice the feel of her body against his. Nissa was his friend, nothing more. And if a part of him wanted to breathe in the scent of her hair or enjoy the way her breasts felt nestling into his chest, he only had to play the "she's Shane's sister" card to make it all go away.

She stepped back. "Again, thank you for taking me in. I'm really happy for Mimi. Of course I am, but wow did it upset my summer plans." She smiled. "Which makes me a horrible person, so don't think about that too much. As I bring in my stuff, I'll work on repairing my character."

"There's nothing wrong with your character, and I'm happy to have you here for as long as you want to stay." He looked past her to the very full car. "Why didn't you ask me to help you move?"

"I was fine." She waved a hand in dismissal. "Shane carted boxes into my storage unit. Those were heavy. This is nothing. I'll just take a few trips to get it all inside."

"*We'll* take a few trips," he told her. "Let me show you to your room, then we'll bring in your things."

She tilted her head. "You didn't have to say yes, you know. Are you sure you're comfortable with me invading your space? I can be messy and I'm not sure we like the same music."

"Stop," he told her, stepping back to wave her inside. "I'm glad you'll be here. I'll enjoy the company and Hilde needs someone to fuss over."

"Hilde was so nice when we texted." Nissa leaned close and lowered her voice. "She asked me what kind of cheese I like. No one's ever asked me that before. I honestly didn't know what to say. I was afraid I would disappoint her if I didn't ask for something fancy, but all I could think of was cheddar."

He thought about the contents of the refrigerator. "She bought more than that. You can try them all and tell her which ones you like best."

"I can't wait." She paused in the foyer and looked up.

He followed her gaze, taking in the two-story entry, the large windows and elegant chandelier. Desmond had lived in the house long enough that he no longer saw any one part of it, but he knew it wouldn't be the same for Nissa. While she'd been to the house a few times for parties and barbecues, she'd never lived here.

She looked at the wide staircase and the long hallway, then back at him.

"Is there a map?" she asked, her eyes bright with humor.

"It's an app."

"I almost believe you."

Hilde, his housekeeper from the day he'd moved in, appeared. She was in her mid- to late-forties, with short dark hair and a warm smile.

"Miss Nissa," she said, her hand outstretched. "Welcome to Mr. Desmond's home. Please let me know if I can do anything to make your stay more pleasant."

"I'm thinking you've already done so much," Nissa told her. "It's nice to meet you in person. I hope you didn't go to too much trouble."

"No trouble." Hilde glanced at him. "Did you want to take her on a tour, Mr. Desmond, or should I do it?"

"Go ahead," he murmured, thinking she knew the house better than he did. But instead of retreating to his office, he joined the two women as Hilde led the way.

"The formal dining room," Hilde said, pausing inside the doorway. "The table expands to seat twenty." She glanced at him. "Mr. Desmond doesn't have any dinner parties. Maybe while you're here you could talk to him about that."

A dinner party? Why would he want to do that?

Nissa glanced at him, her mouth curving into a smile. "I will happily talk to Mr. Desmond about a dinner party. Who should we invite? Ex-girlfriends?"

"Only if your ex-boyfriends come, too," he told her.

"Hmm, I'm less excited about that."

They followed Hilde into the large kitchen. She showed Nissa all the appliances and the pantry. Nissa seemed taken with the six-burner stove and the contents of the refrigerator, especially the cheese drawer.

"Does Mr. Desmond ever come in here?" she asked.

"He does," Desmond told her. "I make my own breakfast every morning and if I'm eating at home, I eat in the kitchen."

There was a very nice table by the window. Or he took his meal back to his office. He was by himself—it made no sense to go sit in the big dining room.

"You can cook?" She pressed a hand to her chest. "I'm genuinely impressed."

He smiled at her. "Gee, thanks."

They toured the rest of the downstairs. The family room and formal living room both had views of the Sound. Nissa stuck her head into his office, and gasped at the size of the laundry room. Upstairs, Hilde showed her the large, well-appointed media room. Nissa stared at the drawer full of remotes, then looked at the giant TV on the wall.

"I could never manage this," she said, shaking her head. "It's too much equipment."

"You can never have too much equipment," Desmond told her. "It's easier than it looks. There's a notebook with instructions in with the remotes."

"Uh-huh. Good luck with that. I'll just livestream on my tablet."

Their last stop was her room. Hilde had prepared one of the suites, with a small living area attached to the bedroom. Both had a Sound view. His housekeeper had done a great job with everything. There were plenty of plush towels in the oversize bathroom and fresh flowers sat on the desk.

Nissa looked around. "This is really nice and much bigger than my condo." She hugged Hilde. "You did far too much work for me, and I want you to know how much I appreciate all of it." She turned to him. "You're being really nice. Thank you."

"Happy to help."

Hilde showed her the laundry chute tucked in the closet. "Just send your clothes down and I'll take care of them."

Nissa shook her head. "I'm going to do my own laundry. You don't have to do extra for me."

Hilde's expression turned stern. "I'll do your laundry."

Nissa raised her eyebrows. "If it's that important to you."

"It is."

She moved next to him. "She's determined."

"Best not to mess with her."

They all went downstairs and outside to Nissa's car. With the three of them working together, it didn't take long to get everything unloaded and delivered to her suite. On the last trip up the stairs, Desmond carried an armful of her hanging clothes. The action felt oddly intimate, as if he were seeing into something private. Silly, really, he told himself. So what if a few of her dresses were draped over his arm?

Once they'd dropped off everything, Hilde excused herself to go start dinner. Desmond hesitated.

"You have the Wi-Fi code," he said, pulling a house key out of his pocket. "Here's this."

She took it. "What about an alarm code or something?"

"It's only set at night. I'll get you the instructions to deactivate it. Or you can ask me."

"But what if you're out on a hot date?"

"I'll probably be home."

"Not seeing anyone these days?"

"No."

She sighed. "Me, either. I'm focused on growing my Italy fund." She waved her hand. "Which you are contributing to by helping me out. Did I say thank you already?"

"Fifteen times."

She grinned. "You'd better get used to it, then. I plan to thank you a lot more."

"You're family, Nissa. And always welcome here."

He chose his words as much for himself as for her. That was what he had to remember. That while she was a beautiful, sexy, smart woman and there was just something about her that got to him, he was not to go down that path. She was someone he needed to look out for and protect, even from himself.

"Thank you." Her gaze met his. "So how does the whole dinner thing work? Is there a bell? Or does a butler show up and escort me?"

"Dinner's at seven. In your honor, we'll be eating in the dining room. After tonight, just let Hilde know if you're going to be home or not. She'll plan meals accordingly."

"You have a great life, Desmond. Next time, I'm going to remember to be rich."

He thought about telling her that his life wasn't what she thought and there were times when he felt isolated and alone. That she was the one with the warm, loving family and to him, that was priceless. But he knew saying the words would be to admit something he wasn't ready to face.

"I'll see you tonight," he told her instead.

NISSA

Nissa got settled quickly. Putting away everything she'd brought with her turned out to be easy,
what with the giant closet with built-in drawers, actual shoe shelves and more hanging space than any
three closets in a normal house. The bathroom was
equally spacious. There were two sinks, drawers between the sinks and a floor-to-ceiling cabinet for
whatever items she might have left over. Oh, and
the toilet not only had a remote control, it lifted the
lid when she walked into the room, as if giving her
a weird toilet greeting.

"I am so out of my element," she murmured as
she plugged in her tablet to charge while she was at
dinner. She wasn't totally sure she could find her
way back to her room after she left, but she was determined to make the effort. Hilde had promised a
special dinner. Given the luxuriousness of the house,
Nissa had no idea what that meant, but she knew it
was going to be good.

By six, she was starving, what with having missed
lunch. She showered and changed into a dress because it seemed that she should. She debated curling
her hair, but that felt like too much, so she settled on
a little makeup, then used up the time until seven by
flipping channels on the TV in her bedroom. Fortu-

nately for her, there was only a single remote and no fancy equipment to worry about.

At six fifty-eight, she left her room and only took two wrong turns before finally making it to the stairs. Once on the main floor, she found her way to the family room where she saw Desmond standing by a built-in bar that had previously been hidden behind concealed doors in the wall.

In the second before he saw her, she used the opportunity to take in his tall, lean body and broad shoulders. Desmond had always been good-looking. Quiet in a confident kind of way, with a thoughtful expression that had made her feel he was really listening when she spoke. A heady occurrence for the younger sister used to being dismissed by her older brother.

Later, as a teenager, she'd thought of Desmond as her brother's cute friend. Interesting and nice, but not, you know, swoon-worthy. That hadn't happened until he'd taken her to prom. A topic she planned to discuss with him, as soon as she found a casual opening.

He saw her and smiled. "You made it."

"I did."

"All settled?"

"Yes, with closet space to spare." She held up a hand. "Before you ask, I have everything I need.

Hilde was very thorough in her preparations. I'm telling you so you can put it in her employee evaluation."

"Good to know." He motioned to the bar. "May I fix you a cocktail?"

"Yes, you may."

She moved closer to the bar and looked at all the bottles on the shelves. "I don't know what most of those are."

"You probably don't want to try them at once. Do you have a favorite drink or may I make a suggestion?"

"Suggest away."

When she went out with her friends, she usually just had a glass of wine or a margarita. Nothing fancy. At her place, she had the obligatory bottle of red wine in her tiny pantry and a bottle of white in her refrigerator and that was it.

As she watched, Desmond pulled out a bottle of rum, along with cranberry juice, a small, unlabeled glass container and a bottle of champagne.

"What's in there?" she asked, pointing at the container.

"Vanilla simple syrup. Hilde made it earlier today." He expertly opened the bottle of champagne.

"So you planned the cocktail you're serving me?"

"I gave it some thought."

"That's so nice. Thank you." She smiled at him.

"You're making me feel special. What if I never want to leave?"

"You're always welcome here, Nissa."

The man had a very nice voice, she thought, his words wrapping around her like a hug. She'd always enjoyed listening to him speak. There was a formality to how he put his sentences together—no doubt the result of a very expensive prep school education.

He mixed the first three ingredients in a shaker, then strained them into a glass and poured champagne on top. After handing her the glass, he waited while she took a sip.

"It's nice. Thank you." She liked the combination of flavors and the fizz from the champagne.

He poured himself a scotch, then they sat across from each other, each on a large, comfy sofa.

She tasted her drink again. "How did you happen to choose this particular drink?"

"I thought you'd like it."

"You have an entire cocktail menu selection handy in your brain?"

"Something like that. Just one of my many skills."

"Because your parents made sure you were prepared for any social situation?"

He nodded.

"So a formal dinner? Meeting the queen?"

He smiled. "Easy."

She raised her eyebrows. "You've met the queen?

And we're talking the actual Queen of England, here. Not Bert, who does a drag show on the weekends?"

He chuckled. "Who's Bert?"

"Don't avoid the question."

He leaned back in his seat and rested one ankle on the opposite knee. "I have met the Queen of England. Twice."

"OMG! And you didn't think to mention me to Prince Harry before he met Meghan?"

"No, I didn't. Did you want me to?"

"Not now! He's married. But before would have been nice. I could have been a princess."

"Technically she's a duchess."

She waved her hand. "One and the same. You disappoint me."

"I apologize for not making your duchess fantasies come true." He studied her, a lazy smile tugging at his mouth. "I wouldn't have taken you for the princess type."

"Nearly every girl is, and let's face it. I'm pretty ordinary."

"I wouldn't say that."

"You're always so nice to me. Thank you. Even when I was an annoying teenager, you made me feel special."

Before she could say anything else, Hilde came into the family room with food on a tray. She set fried zucchini and a luscious-looking dip on the coffee table between them.

"Thank you," Nissa said, eyeing the appetizer. "That looks delicious."

"I hope you enjoy," Hilde said before returning to the kitchen.

Nissa set down her drink and reached for a napkin and a piece of zucchini. "Does she always stay this late?"

"No. Tonight is special. She wanted to be around for your first dinner. She's excited to have someone to fuss over."

Nissa appreciated the sentiment, but felt badly that Desmond's housekeeper was staying late on her account.

"Can you tell her to go home and that we'll serve ourselves?"

"I can try, but it won't work. I've already mentioned that to her. She's not listening."

"If I'm the highlight, you must be a really boring client."

"I think I am. She would be much happier with a family who had a couple of kids and a dog."

"But she doesn't leave you?"

"No. She's loyal."

She took a bite of the zucchini and had to hold in a moan. It was crisp and tender at the same time. The breading flavors were perfectly savory, but when combined with the slightly spicy dip, they were even better.

"This is amazing," she said, reaching for a second slice. "Can we have this every day?"

"If you'd like."

"You're very accommodating. So I'm going to thank you again for letting me stay."

"Will you stop after that?"

"Is it important?"

"Yes. I'm happy to contribute to your Italy fund in this small way."

She laughed. "All right. Thank you and now I'm done. At least for today."

"Good. Have you planned out your trip?"

"A little. I'm hoping to take three weeks. One in Rome, one in Florence and one in Tuscany." She picked up her drink. "And yes, I know Florence is the capital of Tuscany, but it seems as if it's the kind of place that deserves its own week."

"I agree. You should take the trip you want. You've been dreaming about it since you were fourteen."

She had been. A school report on Italy had sparked her interest. Her mother liked to tease her that for an entire year, she'd talked about nothing else.

"How could you possibly remember that?" she asked.

"You found out I'd been there and asked me questions. A lot of questions."

"Was I obnoxious?"

"No. Even then you were charming." He studied her. "You know I could—"

"No," she said firmly. "Just no."

"You don't know what I was going to say."

"I do. You were going to offer to pay for my vacation and while that's very sweet, the answer is no. I want to earn this myself, because that way it's meaningful."

"All right. Too bad you lost the income from Mimi's house-sitting job."

"I know. I'm sad about the money, but happy for her about the baby." At least she tried to be, because it was the right thing to do. But the cash would have been nice, too. "I'll find another job. There's a temp agency I've worked for before. They have very eclectic clients, so that should be interesting."

"You're comfortable having people renting your condo?"

"I wouldn't say comfortable, but they're paying me a lot. I put away everything that's personal, so I'm not freaked about that."

She thought about Shane helping her, which caused her to think about what her brother had said about Desmond and being warned away. Only half a cocktail hadn't given her enough courage to bring up that particular topic.

"What blood type are you?" she asked, reminding herself it was always good to know.

He looked startled by the question. "Ah, A positive."

"Oh, that's not super common. I'm O negative, but I have weird antibodies or something. I can't remember. I'm not a good donor candidate but my blood is very sought after."

"Do I want to know why you know that?"

She grinned. "You forget, I'm a teacher. At my grade level, I teach everything, including science."

Not the reason she'd asked about his blood type, but he would probably accept the explanation. Regardless, she was saved from having to deal with the problem when Hilde appeared and said dinner was ready.

Nissa led the way into the formal dining room where two place settings had been arranged at one end of the table. Desmond poured wine while she admired the beautiful china plates and the fresh flowers. Once they were seated, Hilde brought out tomato gazpacho soup and a basket full of crusty, warm rolls.

"Bread," Nissa breathed, eyeing the temptation. "I love bread." She smiled at the housekeeper. "This all looks wonderful. Thank you so much."

"You're welcome."

Hilde shot Desmond a look that Nissa couldn't interpret. She waited until they were alone to ask, "What was that glance about?"

"I'm sure she was trying to tell me to eat dinner at home more often."

"You don't?"

"Many nights I grab something to-go."

"When you could eat like this?" She took a roll and placed it on her side plate, then tasted the soup. It was the perfect blend of fresh and seasoned with a touch of creaminess.

"I get busy. It's easier than having a set time to be home."

"If you didn't have an empire, you could enjoy your life more."

He smiled at her. "If I didn't have my empire, I couldn't afford Hilde."

"Oh, right. I guess everything's a trade-off. I love my work, but no one gets rich being a teacher."

"Did you want to be rich?"

She laughed and waved her hand at the dining room. "There are obvious perks. But if you're asking if I wish I'd chosen a different profession, no. I love what I do. The kids are great and I really enjoy my days. Do I wish the school district budgeted more money? Of course. But otherwise, I'm a happy camper."

"You're an upbeat person."

"I am. Some of it is my personality and some of it is the joy of annoying others."

He grinned. "Attitude. I like it."

"It's easy to be brave when there's nothing on the line," she told him, only to remember there was a topic she needed to discuss and that waiting for the false courage of alcohol was a flawed plan. If she wanted the information, she was simply going to have to ask the question.

She cleared her throat. "So Shane helped me pack up my grandmother's china."

"You mentioned that."

"Right. While we were doing that, he teased me about living with you and during that discussion he mentioned that back when I was in high school and you took me to prom, that he warned you about me. I mean he warned you to not plan on going out with me. Later. After prom. Obviously we went to prom. Together."

She pressed her lips together, wondering how much of a mess she'd made of that.

Desmond studied her for a second before saying, "He's right."

Was he being difficult on purpose? "About what part?"

"All of it. I enjoyed our evening together and when I mentioned that to him, he reminded me you were a lot younger and less experienced than I was."

"So you should leave me alone?"

"Exactly."

"Which you did."

His dark gaze met hers. "Yes."

"I'm perfectly capable of making my own decisions about who I date," she reminded him.

"Now. Back then you were barely eighteen and I was in grad school. We were in different places."

True, but still. "You had a good time with me, didn't you?" she asked.

One corner of his mouth turned up. "I did. Very much."

"Me, too." She thought about how attentive he'd been, and the slow dancing. And the kissing. The kissing had been spectacular. "You were a great date."

"You, too."

They stared at each other, then his gaze lowered to her mouth. She wondered what he was thinking and if he had any regrets about listening to her brother. If they'd started dating back then they would be... She wasn't sure exactly what, but something. Maybe they would have stayed together all this time.

Desmond looked away. "They say we're in for a warm summer," he said.

Was it just her or was the man the tiniest bit flustered? "Do they?" she asked, hoping she was right and not indulging in a little too much wishful thinking.

Chapter Three

NISSA

After a dinner of pan-grilled chicken with fresh plum salsa and green beans, followed by coconut layer cake for dessert, Nissa and Desmond lingered over decaf coffee. She'd always found him easy to talk to, and tonight was no exception.

"When will you find out about your first temp job?" he asked.

"They'll text me tomorrow, telling me where to be and when. If there's a uniform, I'll swing by the offices and pick it up."

One eyebrow rose. "Uniform? Like at a fast-food place?"

"I don't work in food service. I've tried, but I'm not good at it. A lot of businesses have a shirt they want employees to wear. Even temporary ones. Oh, a few years ago I sold hot dogs down by the aquarium, so that's food. I did okay. There weren't a lot of choices, so that helped." She smiled. "To be honest, I have no idea how servers keep the orders straight. Or carry so many plates at once. Or those big trays. If it were me, everything would go tumbling."

"Then we'll clear the table one plate at a time."

"Probably a good idea."

Hilde had left after she served the main course, telling Desmond she would take care of cleanup in the morning. But Nissa and he had already put everything in the dishwasher and wiped down the counters. All that was left were their dessert plates, forks and the coffee mugs.

He glanced at his watch. "It's getting late. I should let you turn in."

They finished up the last of the dishes, then started up the stairs. She had to admit, it felt strange to be in Desmond's house, going to their bedrooms. She'd only been here a few times for parties and those had all ended with her going home.

"Thanks for dinner," she said when they reached the landing. "It was amazing."

"That's all Hilde," he told her.

"I'll thank her in the morning."

They stared at each other. He had a nice face—all strong lines and chiseled features. She thought about moving closer and, um, what? Kissing him? That could be awkward. If he kissed her back, then what? They went to his room and had sex? She didn't do casual relationships and it wasn't as if Desmond had been secretly pining for her.

When she thought about it, she realized it had been over a decade since their prom date. She'd graduated from college and everything. If he'd been so interested, he could have easily asked her out a thousand different times. Before he met Rosemary, after the divorce. She'd been right here—there'd been plenty of opportunity. But he hadn't. Not even once, which was a pretty clear indication that the man wasn't interested at all. So making a move would be stupid. He would be way too nice in his refusal and she would feel like an idiot. Worse, he might ask her to leave and it wasn't as if she had a bunch of places where she could go.

And just like that, whatever vague fantasy she'd been harboring disappeared with a nearly audible poof.

"All right then," she said with a forced smile. "Good night."

She turned and walked determinedly toward her

bedroom. Lucky for her, she'd picked the right direction and managed to find her way to the familiar space. She closed her door behind her, then leaned against it.

No more Desmond-is-handsome-and-sexy thoughts, she told herself. No more anything, where he was concerned. She was going to live here for two months and she needed to remember that and act like a polite but disinterested roommate. Anything else was a slick, steep road to disaster and no one wanted that.

NISSA

Saturday morning Nissa drove to North Seattle. She stopped for donuts on the way and arrived at her friend's house a little after ten.

The neighborhood had seen a revitalization over the past few years. Rather than tear down and start over rebuilding, most residents were sprucing up their older homes with new windows and roofs, and the occasional second story over the garage. Nissa found parking right in front of the house and looked at the unmown lawn. Before leaving today, she would make a point to run the push mower over the grass.

She hesitated before getting out of her car. She loved her friend, but sometimes the visits were emotionally challenging. A few years before, Marisol had been diagnosed with kidney failure. Everyone had been shocked, Marisol and her daughters most of all.

Nissa had known the family since Marisol had been assigned to be her mentor when she'd first started teaching. They'd become close quickly. Nissa had been there when Marisol's husband and the girls' father had been killed in a car accident. Marisol had helped Nissa when she'd decided to end her engagement. They were best friends who depended on each other.

Nissa got out of her car and walked onto the front porch. She knocked once, then waited. Seconds later the door was flung open as Rylan and Lisandra, ten-year-old twins, greeted her enthusiastically.

"Nissa! You're here."

"Are those donuts? Did you get the maple ones?"

"And chocolate. They're my favorite."

"Yes, yes and yes," Nissa said with a laugh, hugging both girls with her free hand. She stepped inside and saw Marisol on the sofa.

Despite the fact that it was already in the low seventies, her friend had a blanket draped across her lap. Her face was pale, and there were dark shadows under her eyes. The toll of her kidney disease was becoming more and more visible.

"Hey, you," Nissa said, handing the donuts to the girls and crossing to the sofa. She hugged her friend. "How are you feeling?"

"Today's a good day," Marisol said. "Thanks for coming by."

"I haven't seen you in a couple of weeks. I want to

catch up." She looked at the empty mug on the coffee table. "Let me get you some more tea. I'll make myself a cup, as well. Two donuts each for the girls?"

Marisol nodded, then leaned back against the sofa and closed her eyes.

Nissa went into the small kitchen. The house was clean and bright, but on the small side. It could do with a spruce-up of its own, but she knew that wasn't in the budget. So far the insurance was covering all of Marisol's medical bills, but she'd had to stop working at the end of the semester and unless there was a kidney transplant, she wouldn't be returning to work in the fall.

Nissa helped the girls choose their donuts, then put a couple more on a plate and carried them and Marisol's tea back to the living room. She got her own drink and joined her friend on the sofa. The girls finished their donuts and retreated to their room.

"How are you really feeling?" Nissa asked when she had taken a seat.

Marisol shook her head. "It's not bad today. I'm tired, but that's to be expected." Exhaustion was just one of many symptoms she endured.

Marisol reached out and squeezed Nissa's hand. "I don't want to talk about being sick. What's happening with you?"

Nissa smiled at her. "I will accept the change in

topic, but only because it's what you want. I'd rather talk about you."

"I'm boring. Tell me about living with Desmond. You've had a thing for him for years. How is that working out? Are you plagued by illicit thoughts?"

Nissa laughed. "Illicit thoughts? Have you been reading Jane Austen again? His house is wonderful and he's the perfect host. I'm doing fine."

Marisol leaned close. "And the illicit thoughts?"

"Fine. One or two. I can't help it. He's very appealing."

"Maybe you living with him is a sign."

"Or God having a sense of humor," Nissa pointed out. "I was just thinking about this last night and if the man had wanted to date me, he would have done something about it before now. So he doesn't and I'm fine with that."

"If you're sure."

"I am. We're friends. That's all."

Marisol sighed. "But I need to live vicariously through you. It's hard when you're not dating. Do you know what your first temp job is going to be? Maybe you'll meet someone there."

"I'm going to be at a doggie day care for a couple of weeks. I'm not sure about that being a hotbed of dating activity."

Marisol wrinkled her nose. "I'm afraid you're right. Oh, unless one of the dogs has a cute dad.

You could date him. It wouldn't be like at school where dating a parent is against policy."

The girls came into the room. Lisandra had a board game in her hand.

"We decided on Monopoly," Rylan announced.

Nissa smiled. "One of my favorites. I'm in. We'll do that, then I'll take you two to Kidd Valley for lunch."

Marisol was on a special diet that was designed to not stress her body. Nissa would fix that before she took the girls out. After lunch they would go to the park to run off some energy while Marisol rested.

As they set out the game and Marisol counted out the money, Nissa asked, "How's day camp?"

"Good," Lisandra told her. "The other kids are nice. We've been doing a lot of craft projects. In a couple of weeks, we're going to learn how to make movies."

"That sounds like fun."

"It is."

They were good girls, Nissa thought, and they'd already been through so much. First losing their dad, then having their mom get sick. She knew they were scared for her. Without a kidney transplant, she wasn't going to survive a year. When she was gone, Nissa would step in. She'd already agreed to be the girls' guardian.

But that wasn't going to happen, Nissa told herself. Marisol would get her kidney and everything would be fine. It had to be. And if it wasn't, she would be there for the twins, partly because she'd given her word, but mostly because she loved them.

DESMOND

Four days after Nissa moved into the house, Desmond found her presence everywhere. Several pairs of athletic shoes and sandals clustered by the door to the garage. A sweater, a hoodie and a light jacket hung on the coat rack. Magazines and books were scattered throughout the family room. Instead of turning on the television in the kitchen and finding it was tuned to his favorite financial channel, he instead saw *House Hunters International* on HGTV.

She had invaded and while she lived with him, nothing would be the same. A truth that he found strangely appealing. His life was too predictable and boring. While he liked the quiet, he also enjoyed knowing there was someone else under the same roof. And if that someone was as lively and appealing as Nissa, then he was a lucky man.

He walked into the kitchen and found her sitting at the kitchen table, a bowl of cereal in front of her. She had on jeans and a T-shirt from the doggie day care center where she was working. She'd pulled her long hair back into a braid and she wasn't wearing any makeup.

For a second, he remembered her at seventeen—

fresh-faced and beautiful enough to make him ache. He'd enjoyed how she always had something funny to say and that her first instinct was to be kind and thoughtful. Even now, when she saw him, she picked up the remote and hit several buttons.

But instead of landing on the financial channel, the TV changed to a cooking show.

"That's not right," she murmured, before looking at him. "I can't remember the number."

"Or where you put your keys."

She winced. "You heard that yesterday morning?"

"They heard you in New York."

She laughed and handed him the remote. "I was panicked. I didn't want to be late on my first day. I can keep track of my phone and my purse and every-thing else in my life. Just not my keys. It's a curse." She flashed him a smile. "Good morning."

"Morning. How did you sleep?"

"Great. The bed is super comfortable and it's much quieter here than at my place. It's all the land you have. No noisy neighbors getting in at three in the morning."

He walked to one of the cupboards and pulled out a bowl. "There's a shelf in the mudroom. I'm going to put this right there. When you walk in the house, put your keys in the bowl. That way you'll know where they are."

"Isn't it early to be that sensible?"

"It's a solution. Unless you enjoy the drama of nearly being late every morning."

She took the bowl from him and set it next to her place setting. "I really don't. I've always thought it's because I have three bubbles and the keys push me into four."

He poured himself coffee. "Three bubbles?"

"You know, above my head. Like thought bubbles. I can keep track of three things or follow three instructions. But the fourth one pushes out the first one. There's only three spaces. So the work I brought home, my purse, my phone, my keys." She shrugged. "One bubble too many."

"Use the dish. Then the keys don't need a bubble."

"That is really smart. Thank you."

He glanced at her breakfast. "What are you eating? The liquid is gray."

She wrinkled her nose. "It's a protein-enriched cereal with almond milk. Want some?"

"Based on the look on your face when you describe it? No, thank you."

"I'm trying to eat healthy."

"There are better ways to do that."

She put down her spoon. "What are you having?"

"Greek yogurt with fresh berries and granola. Toast with almond butter."

She immediately pushed away her bowl. "Is there enough for two?"

He grinned. "There is. Drink your coffee. I'll make you breakfast."

"I can help."

"Not necessary."

He got out the ingredients and put four slices of bread into the toaster.

"What do you do about lunch?" he asked.

"Hilde made me something to take. I feel guilty, but I'm not going to say no. The woman's an amazing cook."

"She is." He scooped the plain Greek yogurt into two bowls. "How's the job going?"

"I like it. The dogs are great. They each have a different personality. The weather's been nice, so they're outside a lot."

He rinsed fresh blueberries and raspberries. "What about cleanup?"

She laughed. "Okay, yes, that's a part of it, but you forget. I work with kids—I'm used to smelly messes. It's not that big a deal. We run around and play ball. I was with the big dogs yesterday and they get along great. When there's a new dog, the day care has a whole process of getting acquainted. There's a group of dogs that are more shy, so the new ones start there and get to know everyone before moving into their size group."

She sighed happily. "In the afternoon, after a rousing play session, we all relaxed in the shade and took a nap for a couple of hours."

"Even you?"

"I didn't sleep, but I did get to cuddle. It's fun. Makes me think about getting a dog." She shook her head. "Don't say it. I know I can't. I work all day. The poor thing would be trapped in my condo and that's no life. But it's fun to play with everyone else's. I wish I could bring Rylan and Lisandra with me. They would love it."

He set her yogurt in front of her and returned to finish the toast. "Who are they?"

"Oh, my friend Marisol's kids. Ten-year-old twins. They're turning eleven in a few weeks and going into middle school in the fall. I can't believe how fast they're growing. Marisol was my mentor when I first started teaching. We became friends and now we hang out all the time. That's where I went on Saturday."

He'd wondered where she'd gone, but had known he had no right to ask. Funny how quickly he was getting used to having her around.

"They're so strong," she added, dipping her spoon into the yogurt. "Marisol lost her husband a few years ago. She was devastated, as were the girls. It was a hard time."

"How are they doing now?"

Nissa hesitated. "They're dealing. It's always something, isn't it?"

There was something she wasn't telling him, he realized, setting the toast in front of her and taking a seat at the table. Not that he would ask. Her friends were her business.

"They're in summer camp, which they really enjoy. But I was thinking I'd like to plan a couple of activities with them this summer. Something more fun than just lunch and going to the movies."

He could see her freckles and the various colors of blue that made up her eyes. Her mouth was full and soft and there wasn't any part of him that didn't want to kiss her. No, not just kiss. In a perfect world, he would slide her onto his lap. She would wrap her arms around him, maybe straddle him while they kissed. He could already feel the weight of her body and the feel of her mouth as she—

He slammed the door on that line of thought. No and no. But heat had already begun to burn, starting a chain reaction that would end with him hard and unable to stand without revealing his serious lack of control. He needed a distraction.

"Let's take them out on my boat," he said.

Nissa took a bite of her toast. "You have a boat?"

"Yes. On Lake Washington. We can spend the day going around here, or head out through the locks and explore the Sound."

"When did you get a boat? I love boats. Why

haven't you invited me out on it? I thought we were friends!"

He held in a smile. "My apologies. I thought you knew. You are welcome out on my boat anytime you would like. Bring your friends. We'll make a day of it."

"Is it a nice boat?"

He raised one eyebrow. "Have you met me?"

She laughed. "Right. Let me rephrase that. How nice is it?"

"It's about fifty feet long with three guest cabins, a good-sized salon. The area up by the flying bridge is covered, so you don't have to worry about too much sun."

"Fifty feet? I have no idea how big that is, but I'm going to assume I couldn't drive it."

"No. There's a captain."

"Other than you?"

"It's big enough that it requires a skill set I don't have time to develop."

"What about getting a smaller boat you could drive yourself?"

"I've thought about it."

But the larger boat was better for parties. Something smaller would mean just him and a couple of friends and somehow that never seemed to happen. He'd thought when he and Rosemary moved up here, they would have a boat for the two of them, but then they'd split up and he'd relocated by himself.

He paused, telling himself he wasn't as pathetic as that all sounded. He couldn't be.

"So you'd have two boats?" she asked.

He smiled. "There's a dock right here on the property. I could keep the smaller boat close."

"Because the big one is too, um, big to be here?"

"Exactly."

She looked at him. "I keep forgetting about the rich thing. I mean I know it in my head, but I don't think about it when we're talking and hanging out."

"That's a good thing."

"Because you know I'm not in it for the money? Is that a real problem?"

"What do you think?"

"I guess it must be, but even without the money, you're still dreamy." She nibbled on her toast. "If you're serious about the boat, I'd love to ask Marisol if she and the girls would want to come out. But you have to be sure."

He would rather talk about her thinking he was dreamy. What did that mean and did being dreamy mean he could nudge her toward his bedroom?

"I'm sure."

"Thank you. That's very nice. And while you're in a giving mood, may I please have a bit of the garden to play with?"

"I have no idea what you're asking." His garden? For what?

"I miss gardening. My mom and I used to garden all summer long, but she and Dad have moved and I live in a condo, so I never get to dig around in the dirt anymore. I thought while I'm here I could plant some flowers, do a little weeding. You know, play."

"You're welcome to dig away," he told her, not sure why she felt the need to ask.

She didn't look convinced. "One of us should probably talk to your gardener. The landscaping is very beautiful, but formal, and I'm not sure anyone will be happy with me claiming space for random flowers and a tomato plant."

"I'll speak to Hilde," he told her. "She oversees the gardeners."

"Thank you. I love Hilde. She's so good at her job."

"She is. I'd like more Hildes in my life, especially at the office. The person who usually coordinates the company summer party is out on maternity leave and her second-in-command is having trouble handling everything." More than once, he'd thought about bringing Hilde in to manage the project.

"Do you need help?" Nissa asked. "I'm available. I don't know anything about a big corporate party, but I could run errands or help with setup."

Which was exactly like Nissa, he thought. "Thank you. I'll let you know if things spiral out of control."

"If that happens, ask Hilde and I'll be her assistant."

She smiled as she spoke, looking impossibly beautiful, sitting there at his kitchen table. James had been a fool to let her go, he thought.

"Would you like to go to the party?" he asked, surprising himself and, based on her wide eyes, her, as well.

"Sure, if it's okay." She smiled. "I guess if you're the boss, you get to say."

"You might want to recall your acceptance when I tell you my parents will be there."

She brushed away the warning. "I've only met them a couple of times, but they seem perfectly nice. Besides, I've never been to a real office party before. Are there rules? A dress code? Can I wear a hat?"

"Did you want to wear a hat?"

"I don't know. Is it a thing? Like the Kentucky Derby, where all the women wear hats?"

"Your mind is a confusing place. You may wear a hat if you'd like. I'll text you the particulars. In the meantime, I'll let Hilde know about the garden and speak with the captain about some dates to take out the boat." He smiled. "I'm leaving breakfast with a to-do list."

She fluttered her eyelashes. "Then my work here is done."

Chapter Four

NISSA

Nissa drove out onto the street. Despite the heat, she had the windows rolled down, mostly because even she could smell the dog on herself. She loved her doggie day care job, but wow, did she get stinky. She desperately wanted a shower and a change of clothes, but she had a more pressing problem to deal with.

Thirty minutes later, she parked in front of the large building that housed Desmond's company. Right now she needed someone to talk some sense into her and he was the most sensible person she could think of.

She walked inside and was immediately aware of the fact that she was dressed completely wrong. While everyone else had on business attire, she was wearing jeans and a purple T-shirt with a dog logo on the front. Her athletic shoes were grass-stained, her face had smudges, plus the whole smell thing. But she'd come too far to turn back now.

She walked up to the security desk and gave her name. "I'd like to see Desmond Stilling please."

The uniformed man looked doubtful. "Do you have an appointment?"

"No."

She thought briefly about explaining how she and Desmond had been friends forever and that she was currently living with him, but decided against it. The "living together" comment might be misunderstood.

"Maybe you could get in touch with his assistant and give her my name," Nissa suggested.

The security guard did as she requested. Seconds later, his eyes wide with surprise, he allowed her through the security gate and led her to an elevator that whisked her to the top floor.

When the doors opened, an attractive forty-something woman in an elegant suit greeted her.

"Mr. Stilling is in his office. If you'll follow me, Ms. Lang."

"I can do that."

The floors were hardwood, the walls a neutral

color. There were a lot of plants, big windows and a general air of business. Everyone was hurrying or talking or busy on a computer. A few glanced up at her, then turned away before making eye contact. She wasn't sure if that was good or bad.

She and her escort walked through a series of open doors before finally passing an anteroom and a final set of double doors. Nissa stepped inside and saw Desmond behind a large desk. All that was really impressive, but what totally got her attention were the floor-to-ceiling windows. Desmond had an incredible west-facing view of the water and Blackberry Island and the Sound beyond.

He came to his feet. "Nissa. I wasn't expecting you. Everything all right?"

She pointed to the windows. "Did you know you had this? How do you work? It's so beautiful. In the winter, you'll be able to watch the storms blowing in. Wow. Just wow."

Desmond nodded at the woman waiting next to Nissa.

"Thanks, Kathy. I'll take it from here."

Kathy left, closing the door behind her. Nissa shook her head. "This is great. I love it. I'm not really an office kind of person, but if I could work here, it wouldn't be so bad."

"Sadly, most of my employees don't get this kind

of view. But the break room is on the floor below mine and it faces the same direction."

"It was very nice of you to give everyone that space." She rubbed her hands up and down her jeans, then exhaled. "I want a dog."

She took a step toward him. "It's been four days and they're so fun and sweet and affectionate. Dogs are the best. They love with their whole heart and they're so happy to see you and I want one. Or all of them. I need you to talk me down. I keep telling myself what we talked about before. I'm gone too much and my condo is small and this isn't a good time, but it's hard. Just one fluffy dog. Is that too much to ask for?"

He smiled at her. "You don't need me here for this conversation, do you?"

"Yes, I do. That's why I came here. So you could be sensible. It's just I think about going hiking with a dog, or camping, and it would be fun."

"You could take it out on my boat."

Her eyes widened. "Could I? Oh, we could buy one of those doggie life jackets." She shook her head. "No. Stop it. You're not helping."

He sat on the corner of his desk. "You're not getting a dog. Once you move on to another temp job, the need won't be so intense."

"You're killing my dream."

"Your dreams are too big to kill and you know

I'm right. You will probably get a dog eventually, but this isn't a good time."

"I know. But I want one."

"Deep breaths. It's just a couple more weeks."

"I feel pouty."

"What can I do to help? Would you like a hug?"

She would. A nice, squeezy, Desmond hug with her body pressing against his. Of course he was offering comfort and she was hoping to get a little hug action, which wasn't fair of her. Plus, you know, the smell.

She took a step back. "Don't get close to me. I have doggie stink on me. I need to go home and shower. Thank you for reminding me to be sensible. It's just they're so sweet. We never had pets when I was growing up. I should ask my mom about that. Did you?"

"Have pets? No. My parents wouldn't have allowed them in the house. Too much mess. They barely tolerated me."

She smiled as if she got the joke, but she knew in some ways, he wasn't kidding.

"Want me to scold them when I see them at the office party?" she asked. "I will. I have a great scolding voice. It comes from years of being stern when the situation requires it at work."

One corner of his mouth turned up. "While I would pay money to see that, I would never ask you to do that. Besides, that was a long time ago. These days they're far more interested in getting me married."

"Why?"

"They want an heir."

"Because of the empire, right? That makes sense. My parents want me to get married and have grandchildren for them. So it's kind of the same thing."

They looked at each other. She knew he was thinking it wasn't the same thing at all, but he was too nice to say that.

An unexpected and unpleasant thought occurred to her.

"Is me living with you getting in the way of a relationship?"

"I'm between women right now."

Whew. "Is there a waiting list? Or an application process?" she asked, her voice teasing.

"There's a form they fill out online."

She laughed, knowing she liked him a lot. She always had.

"I'm going to go while I'm feeling strong about not getting a dog," she said. "Thank you for your help."

"Anytime. I'm always here for you, Nissa."

She nodded and let herself out of his office. On her way back to her car, she told herself while the words were nice, he only meant them as a friend and not anything remotely more than that.

DESMOND

Unless he had plans to do something with Shane, Desmond usually worked on the weekends. He did so in his home office, but still, there was work. Without interruptions from phone calls and meetings, he could get through a pile of paperwork, review reports and generally get caught up. Not the healthiest decision for himself personally, he acknowledged, but excellent for the company.

But on this particular Saturday, he had trouble concentrating. The cause was obvious—Nissa. Despite the fact that he could neither see nor hear her, he knew she was around. Out in the yard, to be exact, doing whatever it was she planned to do in what she referred to as her "temporary plot of earth."

As he'd suggested, Hilde had talked to the gardeners, who had given Nissa a section of the garden to do whatever it was she wanted to do. Her interest in planting flowers wasn't anything he could relate to, but it was obviously important to her, which meant it was something he would make sure got done.

As long as she was happy, he told himself. While she was living here, she was his responsibility.

He turned his attention back to the spreadsheet on his computer. Three minutes later, he swore softly, saved his work, then closed the program. He wasn't making any progress on the work he'd brought home.

Better to admit defeat and let it go than to keep staring unseeingly at the screen.

He got up and walked through the house to the back door and stepped outside. Typical to the Pacific Northwest, the warm weather had given way to several days of cool temperatures and lots of rain. Today it would barely reach seventy degrees, as they transitioned back to something more summerlike.

The backyard was about an acre of manicured lawn and tidy plant beds. There was a huge pool off the rear deck and beyond that, a stone path led the way down to the dock and Lake Washington. Tall, thick hedges provided privacy on either side of his property.

He glanced around but didn't see Nissa anywhere. He started to circle around the house and found her on the south side, on her knees, using a spade to dig out roots.

She had on jeans and a T-shirt. Her long hair was pulled back in a braid and a big hat covered her head and shaded her face. Gardening gloves protected her hands. Nothing about her was the least bit provocative, but he still found himself moving more quickly as he approached—as if he couldn't get there fast enough.

Just the sight of her made him feel better about the day. He waited for her to look up and smile when she saw him—as she always did—looking forward to the sense of anticipation her smiles always produced.

Before she saw him, she rose gracefully to her feet, then reached for a shovel. He hurried over and took it from her.

She looked up at him and grinned. "Checking up on me? I'm in demolition mode, so don't judge. Later, when the new plants are in, you'll see a riot of color."

"Why didn't you ask for my help?"

She frowned. "For what?"

He waved the shovel. "The heavy work."

"Desmond, I can dig out a few plants. I'm stronger than I look."

"I have no doubt about that, but I'm stronger than you. Tell me what you want dug out."

She shook her head slowly. "I don't know. Are you capable of manual labor?"

"Very funny. Which ones?"

She pointed to a couple of bushes and a few flowers. "Those, please. I don't want to dig out too much. Come September, everything I plant will be taken out and the garden returned to its former glory. I kind of feel bad for your gardening team. There were actual tears when I told them what I wanted to do."

"I doubt any of them cried."

"It was pretty close to that. They weren't amused by my request to have some yard."

He stepped on the shovel, pushing it under the

first bush. With the recent rains, the soil was damp and he dug in easily.

"Do you want me to talk to them?" he asked, lifting the bush out of the ground.

"What? No. I was sharing, not hinting. Come on, Desmond. Look at your yard. It's beautifully designed and maintained. These guys take pride in their efforts and here I am, messing with it. I'm being incredibly self-indulgent. But I can't help it. Digging in the dirt makes me happy." She paused, then laughed. "Actually watching you dig in the dirt isn't bad, either."

"Glad to help."

He made quick work of the plants she wanted removed. Once he was done, they tossed them into the composting bin.

"What's the next step?" he asked, helping her sweep up the path.

"I go buy plants. I talked to my mom earlier this morning and she gave me some good ideas. Because it's already July, I'm not going to be able to grow anything like vegetables, so I'm sticking with pretty flowers that make me happy."

"How is your mom?"

"She's good. She and Dad are going to come over to this side of the mountains in a few weeks to hang out with me and Shane."

"They're welcome to stay here," he said, thinking

it would be nice to spend time with Shane and Nissa's parents. They had always been kind to him, drawing him into the family and including him in their traditions. Around her family, he'd always felt...normal.

"They were going to stay with Shane, but I'll make the offer," she said. "I'm sure he'll be excited." She gave him an impish smile. "Apparently he's still dating his new lady friend. We're talking about four weeks' worth of relationship. You know how rare that is for him. Having my parents bunking in his place will cramp his style."

Desmond chuckled. "I'm happy to help the cause."

She looked at him. "Do you think he's going to get serious about her?"

Desmond hesitated before saying, "Shane hasn't said much to me about her," which was the truth. What he didn't say was that Shane had his reasons for not wanting to commit to anyone. Reasons Nissa didn't know about and that Desmond wasn't going to mention. Shane was his best friend and Desmond would never betray a confidence.

"When are you going to buy plants?" he asked, hoping she didn't notice his attempt to change the subject.

"Right now. Fred Meyer is having a sale," she said, naming a popular local superstore chain.

"Or you could tell the gardener what you want and he could get them from the nursery he uses."

She sighed. "Wow, you really have led a sheltered life. I don't know exactly what I want. I'll wait to see what looks good and appeals to me. Plus, buying the plants is part of the fun. It's satisfying to bring them home and then plant them myself."

"If you say so."

She pulled off her gloves. "You sound doubtful and that makes me feel challenged. All right, you're coming with me to the store. You obviously need to experience the thrill of plant buying." She paused. "Unless you have plans or something."

"No plans." And if he'd had any, he would have canceled them. He would much rather spend the rest of the morning with Nissa.

"Great." She glanced at the tools scattered around. "Let's leave these here. We'll need them for planting later."

Five minutes later they were in her car, heading to Fred Meyer. There had been a brief discussion about which car to take, but she'd insisted on hers, claiming putting plants in the back of his expensive Mercedes would make him weep and she didn't want to be responsible for that. Which was how he found himself in the passenger seat of her Honda CRV.

She chatted as she drove, mentioning the change in the weather and how she was still trying to be strong about not getting a dog. He tried to pay attention to her words but kept getting caught up in his awareness of her. They were sitting close in her car. It would be easy to slide his arm across the console and settle his hand on her thigh.

Or not, he told himself firmly. Nissa was a friend. She was too important for him to mess with that way. Besides, he owed her family. The last thing they would want was her hooking up with some heartless guy.

They pulled into the crowded parking lot. Desmond was surprised at the number of people at the large store. Nissa had to circle a couple of times to find a spot near the nursery.

"Why so many people?" he asked as they got out.

She looked at him over the vehicle. "It's Saturday. People do their shopping on Saturday. Fred Meyer sells food and clothes and home goods, as well as plants. It's a popular and convenient one-stop shopping spot."

He glanced around. "I didn't know that."

"Have you ever been?"

"I don't shop much."

"Or ever. Do you at least buy your own clothes?"

"My suits are custom-made, and my tailor has my measurements." At her look of incredulity, he quickly added, "I have a shopper at Nordstrom who takes care of the rest."

She stared at him. "I forget who you are. To me you're just Desmond whom I've known forever."

Something flashed in her eyes that he couldn't name, but then it was gone. "You're a friend and a part of my life. But there's so much more to you, isn't there?"

He walked around the car until he was standing in front of her. "No. I'm exactly who you think I am."

"With a billion-dollar fortune and a multinational company."

"It's not a billion dollars."

She smiled. "But you're closer to a billion than to a million, right?"

"Maybe." He brushed a bit of dirt off her cheek. "It doesn't change anything."

"Except if you weren't rich, you'd be shopping at Fred Meyer, like the rest of us."

"I'm shopping here today."

She leaned in for a hug. Desmond pulled her close, wrapping his arms around her. She felt good, leaning against him. Warm and feminine. He wanted to do more than hug. He wanted to have her look up at him so he could kiss her. A long, lingering kiss, totally inappropriate for a store parking lot. But she didn't and he knew better than to go anywhere near that sort of thing.

"All right you," she said stepping back. "Let's go buy plants."

She went in through the nursery entrance, pointing at a flatbed cart. "You get to push that, but be careful. No bumping into people. It's not nice."

"Yes, ma'am."

Once they were in the fenced area, she started walking along the aisles of plants, choosing pots of flowers as she went. While he didn't know any of the names, he recognized a lot of them from her mother's garden.

He put the plants on the cart and was mindful of the other customers. But when he saw a small display on the other side of the nursery, he excused himself and went over to study the beautiful plants.

Long, elegant stems supported creamy flowers with purple centers. Nissa joined him.

"Do you like orchids?" she asked.

"Yes. Because of your mom."

"My mom didn't grow them. She loved getting them, but they seemed to be the one plant she couldn't keep alive."

He looked at her. "Your dad brought one home for her the first time I came to visit. Shane and I had just arrived when he walked in with the orchid. Your mom was surprised, but happy, even as she told him it was too expensive and he shouldn't have."

Nissa stared at him. "How do you remember that?"

"I remember everything about my visits to your old house."

He could walk it blindfolded. He knew which stairs creaked and how to jiggle the handle when the toilet got fussy. On Christmas, stockings were opened first thing, followed by breakfast, then the real presents.

"I'd never been in a house like that," he added.

"Small?" she asked with a laugh.

He shook his head. "Normal. You all loved each other. I could see that. Your parents made me feel welcome, maybe for the first time ever. Your mom made me a stocking. I'd never had a Christmas stocking before. Those were the best Christmases of my life."

He hadn't meant to admit all that, but it was too late to call the words back. Besides, he didn't mind Nissa knowing how he felt. Being with her family had always been the best part of his year. He was accepted as just another kid in the house. Her mother had looked out for him and her father had talked to him about life in a way his own father never had.

She reached past him and picked up one of the orchids. "We'll put this in the kitchen and see what happens."

"I'd like that."

Their gazes locked. He felt something pass between them. A connection, he supposed. Shared memories of good times.

She looked away first. "This Christmas you need

to hang your stocking. Otherwise, how is Santa going to fill it?"

He chuckled. "Is that what I've been doing wrong? Thanks for the tip."

"Anytime."

Chapter Five

NISSA

By late afternoon the plants were in the ground and watered. Nissa and Desmond put away the last of the tools. She'd expected him to simply drop off the plants by the path and disappear back into the house, but he'd stuck with her through all the hard work.

"I couldn't have gotten through all this today," she told him. "I would have had a bunch more to put in the ground tomorrow. You were great."

He flashed her a smile that made her insides a little quivery. "I had a good time."

They picked up the last of the tools and put them

in the shed before heading into the house. She was hot and sticky, but satisfied. She was on her way to having fun flowers for summer—temporarily, but that was good enough for now. One day she might be able to buy a house and then she'd have a real garden with vegetables and maybe a cherry tree or two, and all the flowers she wanted.

When they reached the kitchen, Desmond glanced at her. "Hilde left chicken marinating and a few salads. I was going to barbecue. You're welcome to join me if you'd like. Unless you have plans. It's Saturday, after all."

Plans as in a date? Yeah, not so much these days. In fact she hadn't been in a serious relationship since she and James had broken up over two years ago.

"I don't date," she blurted before she could stop herself. "I mean I can, but I don't. Or I haven't been. Um, lately."

She consciously pressed her lips together to stop herself from babbling like an idiot, despite the fact that the damage was done.

"So dinner?" Desmond asked, rescuing her without commenting on her babbling.

"I'd like that. After I shower. Meet back down here in half an hour?"

"Perfect."

There was an awkward moment when they both tried to go through the kitchen door at the same time.

Desmond stepped back and waved her in front of him. She hurried out, then raced up the stairs and practically ran for her bedroom. Once there, she closed the door and leaned against it.

"Talking isn't hard," she whispered to herself. "You've been doing it since you were two. You know how to do this."

But when it came to being around Desmond, knowing and doing were two different things.

She headed for the bathroom, trying to decide what to wear as she went. It was a casual dinner at home. She shouldn't worry about dressing up. But hanging out with her host was anything but casual, which left her in a quandary.

After a quick shower, she discovered that her wardrobe had not become sophisticated or elegant since the last time she'd checked. She'd packed away her work clothes, leaving her with an assortment of jeans, cropped pants, shorts and tops. Oh, and two summer dresses, one of which he'd already seen.

Shorts were way too casual, she thought. Plus, she wasn't as confident about her thighs as she would like. So she settled on cute cropped pants and a co-ordinating tank top, both in bright apple green. She gave her hair a cursory blowout and put on mascara, then decided to call it a win.

She made her way downstairs and found Desmond already in the family room, opening the secret bar.

"What are you in the mood for tonight?" he asked.

"Did you have a suggestion?"

"I thought we'd go old school tonight and have gimlets."

She'd heard of the drink but had never tasted one. "I'm in."

She watched him while he collected botanical gin, limes, a few basil leaves and what she'd come to recognize as simple syrup.

He worked quickly and with a confidence that she envied. No matter the situation, Desmond always seemed to fit in. She did well with friends and in her classroom, but in new situations, she was awkward.

He added ice to a shaker, then measured and poured in ingredients. He'd showered, as well. He had on jeans and a polo shirt. Both showed off his muscled body. The man obviously worked out. She would guess there was a gym in the house—probably in the basement.

He capped the shaker and shook it, then put a strainer on top of each of their glasses and poured. After handing her a glass, he led the way to the sofa.

She kicked off her sandals before sitting down and tucking her feet under her. She sipped her drink. "This is nice," she said. "Very refreshing." She liked the lime with the botanical gin and the hint of basil was unexpected.

"I'm glad you like it." He leaned back against the

sofa. "I texted with your mother. She and your dad are going to stay here when they visit."

She grinned. "And you're okay with that?"

"Of course. I enjoy their company and I'm happy to repay their hospitality."

"Will your parents also be staying here when they come to Seattle?"

A muscle in his jaw jumped. "No. They prefer to stay at a hotel. Separate hotels."

She stared at him. "They're not at the same hotel?"

"No. They haven't been together for a few years now. They were never close but recently they've stopped pretending. My mother spends most of her time in Paris while Dad lives in New York."

"Are you all right with that?"

"My opinion isn't relevant. If you're asking if I'm worried they'll get a divorce, the answer is no. They won't. There's too much at stake. Besides, they each have their lives."

"But not with each other."

"You're thinking they were once in love and now they're not. It wasn't like that with them. They had a merger. It was a sensible decision that grew both businesses. Romance wasn't part of the package."

"That's sad."

"Why? It's what they expected and it's what they got. Even when I was little, they rarely saw each other. They took separate vacations, sometimes bringing me along, sometimes leaving me with my nanny."

She'd known the basics of his past, but not any details. Certainly not that his parents had been so estranged. Or maybe that was the wrong word, because it implied that at one time there'd been a connection.

"I can't understand how anyone would do that," she admitted. "Marry for business reasons."

He looked at her. "Marrying for love is a relatively new idea. For hundreds of years marriages were arranged with economics in mind."

"I wouldn't have liked that. I'm not sure I could go through with an arranged marriage simply for the sake of the family fortune."

"Back then, you wouldn't have had a choice."

"Did your mom?"

"I don't know. She doesn't talk about it. When I've tried to ask questions, she'd always told me she's perfectly content with her life. She also pointed out that her way was far more sensible. Emotions were messy and unnecessary." He raised one shoulder. "Neither of my parents has much interest in feelings. They don't see the point of love and affection. It comes with not having a heart. It's sort of a family trait."

"They have hearts."

"They're not mean or cruel, but they don't believe in love. Duty, yes. That makes sense to them.

But to do something just out of love isn't their way. Or mine."

She finished her drink and put the glass on the table. "I don't accept that, Desmond."

"You should. I've been told I'm quite the heartless bastard more than once."

"Whoever said that was wrong. You care. You love me and my family. I know you do."

His gaze locked with her, making her aware that using the *L* word might have sent the conversation in a direction she didn't want to go.

She cleared her throat. "What I mean is you love us the way you love family. Regular families, not your family. I didn't mean romantically. You're not in love with me or anything. You love us the way we love you."

His mouth twitched as if he were trying not to smile. "Would you like me to change the subject?"

"Yes, please."

"And pretend this never happened?"

"That would be great."

"The Mariners are doing well."

Baseball, she thought with gratitude. There was a safe topic.

"They are. I wonder if they'll make the playoffs this year."

Later, as she put together a green salad and Desmond cooked the chicken, she thought about his comment about not having a heart. He couldn't really believe that, could he? Desmond was kind and generous—of course he cared about people. But she understood why he might want to hold back. His marriage to Rosemary hadn't ended how he'd wanted, and that sort of thing left a mark. She knew she was still dealing with James scars and they'd never even been married. That kind of pain could change a person.

That had to be it, she told herself. Because if Desmond thought he was heartless like his parents, he was the wrongest of wrong.

NISSA

Wednesday after work, Nissa walked into the kitchen to find Hilde at the island, several cabinet doors spread out in front of her.

"What are those?" she asked.

Hilde waved her closer. "We're remodeling the kitchen. Mr. Desmond approved the budget and hired a decorator, but he won't help me make decisions about what to order."

Nissa turned in a slow circle, studying the huge kitchen. She was pretty sure her entire condo would fit in here with plenty of room for a deck or two. The mid-tone cabinets went up to the ceiling and the island was in a good location, but the stove seemed old and the hardware on the cabinets was dated.

"Was anything done to the kitchen when Desmond moved in?" she asked.

Hilde shook her head. "No. Mr. Desmond had his bathroom remodeled and the house painted. New carpet was put upstairs but nothing else. This kitchen is about twenty years old."

"Then it's time. What do you have so far?"

Hilde opened a cabinet and pulled out several appliance brochures, along with paint swatches and three different floor plans.

"I have all this, but it's not my kitchen," Hilde said, sounding stressed. "Mr. Desmond needs to decide and he won't."

Nissa grinned. "Then I'm going to have to explain to him how that's totally unacceptable. Is he in his study?"

"Yes, Miss Nissa. He's been home about half an hour."

Nissa walked down the long hallway that led to Desmond's private study. The door was open and he was sitting at his manly desk, his attention on his computer.

His gaze was intense, she thought as she paused in the doorway. Desmond was the kind of guy who focused on one thing at a time. She allowed herself a few seconds of wondering what it would be like to have all that attention focused on her, then softly cleared her throat.

He looked up and smiled when he saw her.

It was a good smile, the kind that welcomed and told her he was pleased to see her. As if she were important to him. Telling herself not to read too much into his reaction, she leaned against the doorway and folded her arms across her chest.

"You are needed in the kitchen," she said.

"Am I?"

"Yes. You need to make some decisions on the remodel and today is the perfect time."

The smile disappeared. "It's not my thing. Hilde's handling it."

"It's your house and you get the final say. Whether or not it's your thing, it's your responsibility. Come on, Desmond. Look at a few samples. Wave imperially at one of them and we will all rush to do your bidding. You'll like that part of it."

His mouth stayed straight but she saw humor flash in his eyes.

"People do my bidding all day long," he told her. "I don't need it at home."

"Then indulge me." She dropped one arm to her side and raised the other as she pointed down the hall. "Kitchen. Now."

"You're so bossy."

"I can be and that should frighten you."

He got up and followed her back to the kitchen. Nissa held up both hands.

"Ta-da! I bring you Mr. Desmond."

Hilde motioned to the cabinet samples on the island. "We have to pick which one. They're going to be custom-made, so the trim can be changed to how you like."

Desmond studied them. "Any of them is fine."

Nissa moved close. "Don't say that. You have an opinion. Door style. Simple? Ornate? Something in between?" She pointed to a Shaker style. "I think that's too plain, but you don't want anything really fussy. This is a big kitchen and there are going to be a lot of cabinets."

Desmond looked at the doors, then out the big windows toward the backyard.

"This part of the house faces more north than east, so there isn't as much natural light. So nothing too dark."

He moved closer to the cabinets and studied them.

"This detail," he said, pointing at quarter-round trim. "No inlay."

They discussed other possibilities before Desmond chose the ones he liked best. From there the discussion moved on to appliances. Hilde made a case for a warming drawer.

"I've always wanted one," she admitted. "They're so nice for entertaining, and in the winter. It's no fun to put hot food on a cold plate. My mom bought me a silly plug-in plate warmer. It's like a folded heating pad. While it works, a warming drawer would be pretty amazing."

Desmond nodded at Hilde. "A warming drawer it is. What else?"

"The stove." Hilde fanned out several brochures. "I like this one best. It's big and a little more expensive but it has two ovens and a grill."

Desmond nodded. "I like the grill. I can barbecue in the winter."

"Yes, and it changes out to a griddle. I would use that a lot."

He refused to weigh in on which refrigerator, so Hilde and Nissa discussed options. When it came to the layout, all three plans worked, but one involved a lot more construction, basically turning the kitchen ninety degrees.

"I don't think it's worth it," Nissa said. "It's a lot more work and money, and for what? To me, everything is where it belongs right now." She smiled at Hilde. "But your opinion is more important than mine. You're the one who works in this kitchen."

Hilde tapped one of the other designs. "Yes, I agree. Why make so many changes? I like how things are now. It just has to be refreshed."

Hilde and Desmond studied the other options before picking one. After that they moved on to paint colors and made their choices very quickly. When they were done, Hilde made a final list of their choices.

"Thank you, Mr. Desmond. I'll call the decorator in the morning."

"You're welcome, Hilde. I shouldn't have waited so long to get involved."

Nissa walked him back to his office. "That was fun. I love spending other people's money."

"I appreciate your help." He walked into his office, then turned back to her. "I was wrong to push that all on Hilde. She wasn't comfortable making the decisions herself."

"Plus you're her boss, and she has to think about that. I, on the other hand, am free to annoy you whenever I want."

"You're never annoying."

"Really? Because sometimes I try to be."

He smiled. "No, you don't. You're easy to be around. I like that."

Was that the same as liking her? Like as in like-like? Because she knew Desmond liked her as a friend, but was there anything else she should know about?

He started for his desk, then paused. "Are you still up for the company party?" he asked. "My planner was asking about my plus-one."

"I'll be there. I'm looking forward to meeting

your staff and telling them what you were like as a teenager."

He chuckled. "I'm not worried. There are no secrets in my past. Besides, if there were, I would trust you to keep them."

"I totally would. Except for the embarrassing ones." She paused, not sure what to say next. It seemed like they were almost going somewhere, but maybe that was wishful thinking on her part.

"Dinner at seven?" she asked instead.

"I'll be there."

Two weeks into living with Desmond, Nissa had settled into a routine. She went to work—she was still at the doggie day care—came home, showered, had dinner with Desmond and then retreated to her spacious room where she relaxed with an audiobook or watched something on one of the streaming services he made available to her.

She'd gone over to see Marisol and the girls every weekend and kept in close touch with her friend. Shane kept talking about getting together, but so far he claimed to be too busy with work, which she took as code that he was still involved with his mystery woman. If the relationship went on much longer, she was going to have to do some serious investigating. In the meantime, she had a party to get ready for.

Mid-July meant summer sales, so she'd indulged

in a mini shopping trip. She'd bought a new summer dress for the event—a pretty black fit-and-flare style that fitted perfectly. She already had fancy sandals and a cute evening bag she'd bought years ago.

She took the time to curl her long hair. Actual curls didn't last, but she ended up with waves that looked great. Exactly at six, she went downstairs to meet Desmond.

His summer office party didn't start until seven, but he'd said he wanted to get there early and she'd been fine with that. They would drive there and back together—something that made sense, given their living arrangement. It wasn't a date, she told herself as she reached the main floor. It was convenience. Kind of like carpooling. There weren't any—

"You look beautiful."

She turned toward the voice and saw Desmond in the archway by the dining room. He had on dark pants and a dark gray shirt—nothing special and yet the sight of him made her heart beat just a little faster than usual.

"Thank you," she said, her gaze locking with his. "I wanted to look nice for your work friends."

"Mission accomplished." He motioned to the door. "Shall we go?"

Her nerves continued to be on edge, even as she settled next to him in his fancy Mercedes. Her throat was dry and her skin felt hot, which didn't make sense. This was Desmond. She *knew* him. They were friends. She would trust him with her life. More important, she would trust him with her family, so what was the big deal?

Rather than answer the question, she decided to distract herself with conversation. "Hilde's very excited about the party. You were sweet to invite her and her husband."

"I thought she would enjoy the event."

"She said last year's party was wonderful. Apparently there's dancing."

He glanced at her, his mouth curving into a smile. "I heard that."

"Do you dance with the office staff?"

He returned his attention to the road. "No. But they often dance with each other."

"You must have to balance issues like that," she murmured, watching him merge into traffic as they headed south on I-5. "Being a concerned boss, but not getting too involved. Being in charge without being a mean boss."

"Maybe I am a mean boss."

"I don't believe that. You wouldn't be. You care about people."

"I try to be fair."

She smiled. "See. You can't help it. I'm excited about seeing your parents."

He spared her another glance. "Are you sure about that?"

"Okay, excited is strong, but they've always been really nice to me. Plus, it's fun to see what your mom is wearing. Evelyn has amazing fashion sense and the jewelry is spectacular."

"I wouldn't have thought of you as the jewelry type."

She laughed. "Why would you say that? I don't have much because I can't afford it and if I have extra money I want to save it, but that doesn't mean I don't like sparkly things as much as the next girl."

She thought about the last time she'd seen Desmond's mother. It had been at his housewarming party a couple of years ago.

"That diamond necklace she wore," she said, thinking about how it had glittered. "I doubt I could afford the insurance on it."

"It's probably heavy and uncomfortable to wear," he teased.

"I would be willing to suffer. See how much character I have?"

They talked easily for the rest of the drive. As they approached Seattle, the traffic got heavier. Desmond drove into the city and made his way to the Chihuly Garden and Glass, where the party would be held. He pulled up to the valet parking he'd arranged, then helped her out of the car.

"I've never been here," she admitted, looking at the building in front of them. "I should have come. I always meant to. I'm a huge fan of his work. Did you know there's a massive Chihuly installation in Montreal? It's made of all these individual pieces and every year they have to take it apart and bring it in for the winter."

"I didn't know that, but I'm not surprised. His work is all around the world."

They walked toward the entrance.

"I'm going to stay up front so I can greet everyone as they arrive," he told her. "You're welcome to explore the museum, if you'd like. It's closed to the public for the party, so you'll pretty much have it to yourself."

"I'd love to look around. Thanks for the suggestion."

She really did want to explore and she knew standing with him while he welcomed his guests would only invite a lot of questions. It wasn't as if she and Desmond were a couple. She was just a family friend.

They went inside. He excused himself to go talk to his staff while she collected a brochure on the museum and prepared to be dazzled. But just before she stepped into the first room, she glanced back at Desmond. He'd gone out of his way to make the evening special for those who worked for him. Not exactly the actions of a man who had no heart.

Chapter Six

NISSA

Nissa spent over an hour admiring the various installations. While she'd started out as the only admirer, by the time she entered the outdoor garden the party was in full swing and there were people everywhere. Several smiled at her, but no one came over to talk to her, making her realize that except for Hilde, she didn't know anyone who worked for Desmond. Not that it mattered, she told herself. She was capable of starting a conversation herself.

She took a glass of champagne from a server and looked around, searching for a likely prospect.

Her gaze settled on a familiar older couple. Evelyn and Charles Stilling looked like what they were—wealthy, cultured and well traveled. She knew that each of them had inherited a part of what had become Stilling Holdings, forming the bigger company when they'd married. What she hadn't known until recently was that marriage had been about business rather than affection.

Now she studied them, wondering how they could survive so many years in a loveless marriage. She wouldn't like that at all. For her, marriage was about giving her heart to one man for the rest of her life. She wanted a traditional family with kids and pets and camping.

Evelyn turned toward her and the light caught the spectacular sapphire necklace she wore. Nissa smiled. Okay, maybe she would add a few jewels to her wish list.

She was still smiling when Evelyn glanced in her direction. The older woman studied her for a second before heading in her direction. Nissa moved toward her, as well.

"I don't know if you remember me," she said, holding out her hand. "We've met a few times. I'm Nissa Lang, Shane's sister."

"Yes, of course."

Evelyn had dark hair and eyes. She was tall, slim and moved with a grace that Nissa envied. Maybe she'd studied ballet or maybe she was blessed with natural grace. Nissa wasn't exactly clumsy, but she didn't have anything close to Desmond's mother's style.

"How was your trip to Seattle?" Nissa asked.

"It was commercial travel. One does the best one can, under the circumstances." Evelyn sipped her champagne. "Are you here with Desmond?"

"You mean as a date?" Nissa tried to ignore the sudden surge of nervousness. "No. I came with him because it was easier. I'm staying with him for a few weeks while my condo is rented out." She held in a groan. Really? She'd had to say *that*? "It's not anything romantic. We're friends. Just friends. We have been forever. Desmond would spend Christmas with my family, which, um, I guess you knew because he wasn't with you."

She forced herself to stop talking and offered a tight smile.

Evelyn's expression sharpened. "You're living with him."

"I'm staying at the house. In my own room. Not, you know, *with* him." She made little air quotes, then wished she hadn't.

"So, have you seen the exhibit?" she asked brightly, hoping to change the subject.

"I don't need to. Dale and I are friends."

Dale? As in Dale Chihuly? Sure. She wasn't even surprised.

"Do you think you're right for him?" Evelyn asked bluntly. "You're hardly his type and you bring nothing to the table. How will you help him with business? Be an asset when he travels? What kind of a hostess will you be?"

Nissa went cold. "What are you talking about?"

"It's obvious you have feelings for him. I'm not sure what your ridiculous charade is about staying with him, but not *with* him." Evelyn copied her air quotes. "Desmond always does the right thing. He made a mistake with Rosemary, but he rectified it immediately and he never looked back. She begged for a reconciliation, but he wouldn't have any part of her, once he recognized her for what she was. The same thing would happen with you, Nissa.

"You're the kind of girl who expects love when you marry. Desmond's incapable of that. I consider that a point of pride, but I doubt you'd agree." Desmond's mother offered her a cold smile. "He knows what's expected from him and he will do as we ask. Silly girl. I almost feel sorry for you."

With that, she turned and walked away, leaving Nissa feeling embarrassed and exposed, although she couldn't begin to say why. Although she knew it was her imagination, she felt as if everyone was staring at her, judging her. She felt awkward and out of place and wished that she could be anywhere but here.

She glanced around, looking for an exit and if not that, at least somewhere to hide. She'd barely taken a step when Desmond appeared in front of her.

"Are you all right?" he asked, sounding concerned.

"I'm fine."

He stared at her. "I saw you talking to my mother. What did she say?"

"About what?"

"Nissa, you went white."

Oh no! She couldn't tell him what Evelyn had said—she couldn't talk about it with anyone. "That must be a trick of the lighting. I'm fine."

His dark gaze never wavered. "You don't usually lie to me."

Obviously he got his bluntness from his mother, she thought, wishing she could see humor in the moment, rather than feeling uncomfortable.

"Maybe just this once you could let it go," she told him.

He surprised her by nodding. "Are you hungry?"

"Not really." Her stomach was too upset for her to eat.

"Then come with me."

He took her hand in his and drew her back inside. There was a large dance floor set up under the glass roof. A band played and several couples were dancing.

He took her half-empty champagne glass from her and set it on a table, then pulled her into his arms and started moving them to the music.

At first she could barely follow his movements. She was acutely aware of everyone around them, and worried that his mother was watching. But gradually the heat of Desmond's body, the feel of him holding her, made her relax. She told herself she would deal with her conversation with his mother another time and that she should simply enjoy the rest of the evening.

One song became two and then three. Finally Desmond drew her to the side and found a couple of empty chairs. They sat down.

"That was nice," she said, smiling at him.

"It's like prom."

"Yours?"

He looked at her. "No. Yours. Everyone is dressed up. You look amazing."

"Look at you with the compliments." She tried not to think about what his mother had said—that Desmond was incapable of love and she was silly. "It was a long time ago."

"But still a good night."

"Yes, it was." She'd been so crazy about him, she thought, remembering how the evening had gotten better and better. The best part had been him kissing her at the end. Wonderful sexy kisses that had made her think a future was possible.

"And then you walked away from me," she added softly.

"You know why."

"Imagine where we would have been if you hadn't."

She hadn't meant to say the words, but somehow she had. Desmond's gaze sharpened.

"You mean if we'd kept seeing each other?"

She nodded. "I think about that sometimes."

"So what happens?"

"We'll never know."

He started to speak, then suddenly looked away and came to his feet. One of his assistants walked over.

"A few of the guests are getting ready to leave," she told him. "You wanted me to let you know when that happened so you could say goodbye."

"Thanks, Brittany."

The woman nodded and retreated the way she'd come. Nissa stood. "Go play the host. I'll be fine."

"I won't be long." He pointed to the buffet. "Eat something. You have to be hungry."

"I will."

He turned away, took a step, then spun back to her. Before she knew what was going to happen, he pulled her close and kissed her. The brief contact seared her skin and sent liquid desire pouring through her, but before she could react in any way, he was gone, following Brittany to where his guests were leaving.

Nissa stood there for a couple of seconds, not sure what had happened or how she felt about it. She smiled. Scratch that last thought, she told herself. She knew exactly how she felt about Desmond kissing her. She felt good. And if it happened again, she was going to enjoy every second of it.

DESMOND

Desmond left work nearly two hours earlier than usual. There was no reason—no pressing appointment or phone call. Instead he went home because he knew Nissa was there and he wanted to spend time with her.

He tried to tell himself she would still be there when he left at his usual time, but for some reason the words had no effect. Normally he was disciplined to the point of annoying his friends, but not today. Not with her.

He arrived home a little after four and walked into the house. Nissa was in the family room, the TV on and tuned to a local news show, although the sound was off. She was sitting on the sofa, her hair still damp from her shower. She was reading something on her tablet, wireless headphones on her head.

She was wearing shorts and a T-shirt. Conventional clothing that shouldn't have stirred anything inside of him, and yet did. Or maybe the problem wasn't the bright yellow T-shirt, but the woman wearing it.

He wanted her. Knowing it was a mistake, that he shouldn't cross that line did nothing for the need that lived inside of him. He wanted her and the brief kiss the night of the party had only made that wanting increase.

He thought of crossing to her, of tugging her to her feet and then pressing his mouth to hers until she wrapped her arms around him and begged him to take her to his bed. Assuming Nissa begged. He wanted to know. Was she quiet or did she moan? Was she shy or adventurous? He wanted to learn every inch of her body and discover all the ways he could pleasure her, then he wanted to do it all again, simply because he could.

And then what? He could imagine taking things that far, but the next step always eluded him. What if she fell in love with him? She would want roses and a happily-ever-after. While he could give her the former, the latter wasn't possible.

He remembered when he'd been twelve or thirteen. His parents had sat him down for what they'd billed as "an important conversation." He'd been horrified they were going to talk about sex, but instead they'd explained about his responsibilities to the company. How he was expected to excel at business and build upon what he would inherit.

To that end, he was expected to marry appropriately. A young woman of note, perhaps with a small fortune or another firm worth acquiring. Love was for others, not for him. He could date whomever he wanted, but to take things further was unthinkable. He was to always make the sensible choice, to leave emotions for those who lived smaller lives. He remembered his mother turning to his father and smiling.

"We don't have to worry about Desmond. He doesn't feel things very strongly. He hardly has any friends and no real connections."

She'd said it with such pride. He remembered thinking the reason he didn't have friends was because he was tutored at home. He wanted to be like the other boys he saw through the mansion windows.

Then he'd been sent to boarding school where he'd discovered making friends was harder than he had thought. He'd never fit in, until he'd met Shane. Even though they'd stayed close for the past twenty years, he couldn't help wondering if his mother was right. If there really was something wrong with him. An inability to connect the way everyone else did.

He hadn't wanted that, but no matter how he tried, he couldn't seem to feel the things others did. He might put on a decent show, but the truth was, he was more like his parents than he wanted to admit and in the end, his lack of heart would destroy Nissa. And that was the one thing he refused to do.

So instead of acting on his need, he forced a smile and walked into the room, loudly calling her name. She looked up and smiled at him.

"You're home early," she said.

"I ran out of work."

"I doubt that." She put down her tablet and removed her headphones. "Why don't you go get changed and I'll make tonight's cocktail? I looked online and think I found a good one."

"I look forward to it."

Ten minutes later he was back downstairs. She was in the kitchen, muddling mint in a shaker. As he watched, she poured in simple syrup, rum, lime juice and some kind of puree. After shaking, she added club soda, then poured the drink over ice.

"A pear mojito," she said proudly. "I know it's not your usual thing, but it got great reviews."

"I'm sure I'll like it."

They touched glasses. Nissa pointed to the deck.

"Let's sit outside. The temperature is perfect. Hilde made enchiladas for dinner. We only have to heat them in the oven. There's a delicious salad, too. I'm super excited."

"About Mexican food?"

She grinned. "It's my favorite. I think I was born in Los Angeles in a previous life."

He chuckled as he followed her outside. They sat next to each other on the lounge chairs in the shade. The temperature was in the low eighties and the lake beyond was calm with only a hint of shimmer from the sunlight.

"Tell me about your day," he said, sipping the mojito. It was surprisingly refreshing.

"It was good. I miss the dogs, but delivering flowers doesn't leave me so stinky at the end of my shift. Some of the arrangements are really heavy, which I didn't expect." She flexed an arm. "I'm getting a workout."

"Are they too heavy?"

She raised her eyebrows. "Do not even think about trying to rescue me," she told him. "I'm perfectly capable."

"I know you are, but I want to make sure—"

She held up a hand to silence him. "No. I can do this."

"All right. You delivered heavy flowers. Anything else?"

She laughed. "I'm discovering I don't know the area as well as I thought. There are little streets I've never heard of. But I have GPS on my phone and that makes it easy. Siri loves telling me to make a U-turn because I've gone the wrong way."

"She does have attitude. Do you want to become a florist?"

She looked at him. "Why would you ask that? I love being a teacher."

"I know but when you were working at doggie day care, you wanted to get a dog. I wondered if the trend would continue."

"I might want to plant more flowers in the garden, but I'm going to stick with my current profession." She paused and took a sip of her drink. "What else? Oh, I talked to my friend Marisol today and mentioned the boat thing again. She said she was excited about it. Assuming you're still willing to play host."

"I am. When would you like to go?"

Nissa hesitated. "She hasn't been feeling well for the past couple of weeks, but she's better now. Still weak, but better. How about Thursday? I know it's a weekday, but I have it off and the girls don't have camp that day."

She looked so earnest, he thought, meeting her gaze. Like she was worried about asking for too much. How could she not know that he would give her anything?

"Let me text the captain and see if he's available then," he said, pulling his phone out of his pocket and typing. When he was finished, he looked up. "How old are her daughters? Do you know how much they weigh? We'll want the right size life jackets for them."

She gave him the information and he texted that, as well. Seconds later, Captain Pete wrote back saying he was available and looking forward to it. They settled on a time. When Captain Pete asked about lunch, Desmond suggested the usual picnic fare.

"We're set," he said. "Let's leave at ten and stay out until two or so. Remind everyone to wear sunscreen and bring a hat. We'll have lunch on the boat. The weather is going to be good and the winds will be calm, but if there are any upset tummies, we'll just head back."

She looked at him. "You're very good to me, so I spend all my time thanking you."

"No thanks necessary. I'm looking forward to it." Not just spending time with Nissa, but meeting her friend. He knew a person could learn a lot about someone by how they were with their friends.

NISSA

Nissa tried to relax as she drove to Marisol's house. After several really bad days, Marisol was finally feeling better, but Nissa knew that could change at any second. Happily, when she got to the house, her friend was up and dressed, looking pale but determined.

Lisandra and Rylan practically danced around her, asking questions, one after the other.

"Is it a really big boat?"

"Does it go fast?"

"Mom says the toilet is different—more like an airplane toilet, but we've never been on an airplane, so will we know how to flush?"

"Will we eat lunch on the boat? Can I have a soda?"

Nissa gathered them close and hugged them. "I'm glad you're excited. I am, too. I've never seen the boat, so I can't answer your questions, but we're on our way to the marina right now, so you can see it for yourselves."

Marisol laughed. "They've been like this for two days. I'm amazed they got any sleep last night." She looked at Nissa. "Thank you for arranging this. It's a great distraction for all of us."

"I'm excited, too. Apparently the boat is very fancy."

Marisol raised her eyebrows. "I'm more interested in meeting Desmond. I've been hearing about him for years."

Nissa tried not to flush. "Yes, well, he's a good guy and we're friends."

As Marisol knew about Nissa's ongoing crush, the post-prom debacle and pretty much everything else on the Desmond front, she wasn't likely to buy the whole "friend" thing, but the girls would and that was what mattered.

It didn't take long to collect their tote bags and confirm everyone was protected with sunscreen. They all piled into Nissa's car and she headed for the marina.

She carefully followed the instructions Desmond had given her and was soon entering a code to unlock the big gates that protected the parking lot of the fancy boat section of the marina. There was a big clubhouse, a bar with plenty of outdoor seating and dozens and dozens of boats. Maybe hundreds of them, neatly pulled into slips, bobbing slightly in the water.

She wanted to say there were big boats and small boats, but there weren't. Everywhere she looked were massive seagoing vessels that had to be multiple times bigger than her condo, or Marisol's house.

In the back seat, the girls went quiet and next to her Marisol sucked in a breath.

"He owns one of those?" her friend asked.

"I guess so."

She pulled in next to Desmond's Mercedes, then texted him that they had arrived. He replied that he would be right out. Everyone got out of her car and collected their bags as she saw a gate open and Desmond walk toward her.

She looked at the man multiple times a day—they were living together, so she shouldn't be surprised by his appearance. But there was something about his casual dress—board shorts, a Hawaiian shirt and boat shoes—that made her shiver just a little.

Marisol stepped close. "You didn't say he was so handsome."

"I did."

"You weren't specific enough. The man is hot. How do you resist him?"

Nissa sighed. "If he ever asked the question, I wouldn't, but so far, he's showing amazing self-control."

"Men can be so stupid."

Nissa smiled. "Tell me about it."

When he had joined them, she made introductions. He insisted on carrying their bags as they went inside the gate and onto the ramp that led down to the boats. Marisol went slowly, hanging on.

"Is the walk too much?" Nissa asked anxiously.

"The exercise is good for me."

They passed several boats on their way to the end of the small pier, stopping in front of the one on the end. It was big and sleek, with a dark blue hull. There was a huge covered deck up what felt like three stories, and a bigger open space out back. Large windows allowed them to see a living room and dining area. Smaller windows were darkened so she couldn't see in. Those were probably the bedrooms, she thought, unable to take in how incredibly massive and beautiful the boat was.

"Welcome aboard," Desmond said, waving toward the five stairs that led to the side of the boat. "I'll give you a tour, then we'll get everyone fitted for life jackets and have a quick safety talk before we head out."

Marisol was still hanging on to the pier railing. She looked at the narrow stairs and the gate on the side of the boat, then shook her head.

"I don't think I can do that," she said quietly. "I'm feeling better, but I'm not sure it's possible." She glanced over her shoulder. "Why don't I wait at the clubhouse?"

"Mom," Lisandra and Rylan said together, their voices thick with disappointment. "You have to come. It won't be fun without you."

"I have to agree with them," Desmond said, passing the totes to Nissa and walking over to Marisol. "Do you trust me?"

Marisol's brown eyes widened. "I'm not sure what that means."

"Do you trust me?"

Marisol's expression turned doubtful. "I guess."

Before she could say anything else, Desmond swept her up in his arms. Marisol shrieked and wrapped her arms around his neck.

"What are you doing?"

"I would have thought that was obvious."

He moved to the stairs and took them easily, then stepped over the side of the boat and set Marisol on the deck, before turning to the girls and waving them onboard.

"Come on. We don't want to leave without you."

The girls scrambled after him. Nissa followed, taking the stairs before stepping through the gate and onto the boat.

She immediately felt the movement of the boat—a physical reminder that they were on water. Excitement blended with anticipation as she wondered how great it would be when they were actually moving!

Desmond kept his attention on Marisol. "You doing all right?"

"I am." She studied him. "Now I know what Nissa was talking about."

Nissa didn't know what her friend meant, but decided to go with it. She set their totes on a padded bench as Desmond started the tour.

As she'd seen from the outside, there was a very large living area, a "salon," Desmond called it. The kitchen or galley was much bigger than she would have thought and there were three small bedrooms and two bathrooms onboard.

They returned to the rear deck and were introduced to Captain Pete, a small, wiry man in his fifties.

"Welcome aboard," he said cheerfully. "Who might these young mermaids be?"

Both girls giggled as they introduced themselves.

"Nice to meet you both." Captain Pete leaned close. "So I have some work to do before we can get underway. It would go a lot faster if the two of you would like to help me."

The twins nodded eagerly. Pete led them to the finger pier and started explaining about the lines holding the boat in place. Desmond looked at Marisol.

"I thought we'd spend the day on the upper deck. There's plenty of cover so the girls will be out of the sun. There's a nice breeze and the view can't be beat."

Marisol put her hands on her hips. "You're about to tell me you're going to carry me again, aren't you?"

"I was going to ask rather than tell, but yes."

Marisol glanced at Nissa and mouthed, "He's a keeper," before turning to Desmond. "You're a good man. Thank you."

Desmond carried her upstairs. Nissa followed and found herself on a big, covered deck with plenty of seating, and tables to hold food and drinks. There was a sink, a refrigerator and a stack of towels.

"This is really nice," she said, looking around. "I think I'm in love."

Desmond settled Marisol on one of the bench seats, making sure she had plenty of pillows.

"It's a good boat."

"It's a luxury yacht. How far can it go?" she asked. "Could we sail up to Canada?"

"Probably not today, but she's capable of making the trip."

Nissa thought about what it would be like to spend a few days on the yacht. From what she'd seen, everyone would be really comfortable. Of course the quarters might be a little tight with Captain Pete along. Assuming she and Desmond went as more than friends.

Not that he'd made any moves on her. There had been one brief but mighty kiss and nothing since. A fact that left her confused and wondering if it had simply been a friendly kiss and she'd been wrong to read more into it.

"We have to work on our communication skills," she murmured to herself.

The girls raced up the stairs to the upper deck.

"We saw the engine room and got fitted for our life jackets," Lisandra said.

"The ropes are called lines and the bathroom is called a head," Rylan added. "Captain Pete said once we're underway, we can both steer!"

Captain Pete joined them and made sure the adults knew where their life jackets were, then gave a brief safety lecture. After that, Desmond joined him on the main deck. The powerful engines roared to life and shortly after that, they were off.

The day was perfect—warm and sunny. The girls spent part of their time upstairs with their mom and the rest of it with Captain Pete who was more than patient with their endless questions.

Marisol and Desmond talked as if they'd known each other for years. Nissa listened as her friend expertly extracted information on Desmond's childhood and business. When it was time for lunch, he carried Marisol down to the dining area in the salon.

There were different kinds of sandwiches and salads, cut fruit with dip and potato salad, along with pitchers of lemonade and ice water. Marisol admitted she had an appetite, something that didn't happen much these days.

"It must be the fresh air," Marisol said with a laugh. "I haven't felt this good in a long time."

Rylan put down her sandwich and pulled her hair back in a ponytail. "Look how long it is," she said to Nissa. "Fourteen inches from my fingers." She turned to Desmond. "I need to get to sixteen inches before it can be cut off."

"Me, too," Lisandra added. "My hair's that long, too."

Nissa leaned toward him. "They're growing out their hair so they can donate it. There's an organization called Wigs for Kids. Fourteen inches is good, but sixteen is better."

"That's a big commitment," he told the girls.

"Donations are important," Rylan said. "We want to help."

Nissa wondered if she would say more and confess how Marisol was waiting for a kidney. Nissa still hadn't explained why she was sick—it wasn't her secret to tell—and so far Desmond hadn't asked.

"I know you're doing a good thing," Marisol said, fingering her daughter's hair. "But I'm probably going to cry when they cut it off."

"I'm not," Lisandra said proudly. "I'm going to be brave."

"You already are."

NISSA

After lunch they continued their journey around Lake Washington, then went through the Montlake Cut to Lake Union in the center of Seattle. They dodged paddleboarders and saw a seaplane take off. By two, the girls were sleepy and Marisol looked ready to go back. Captain Pete turned the boat so they were headed for the dock.

Nissa moved next to Desmond on the benches.

"This was wonderful," she said. "We've all had a great time."

"Me, too," he said, gazing into her eyes. "I don't get out on the water enough."

"You should do it more. It's fun."

"That could be the company as much as the boat," he told her.

Which sounded great but made her wonder if there was one person's company he meant in particular, and if so, hopefully that person was her.

Chapter Seven

NISSA

Nissa couldn't remember the last time she'd had such a busy social life. Normally she was a stay-at-home kind of person. Once she'd finished at work, she tended to like going to her condo and settling in for the evening. Oh, there were the occasional drinks out with girlfriends or dinner at Marisol's place, but for the most part, she lived a pretty quiet life.

Lately, though, she was going and doing. Just in the past week there had been Desmond's work party, then a day out on the water, and now she was once again curling her hair and pulling out her new party

FREE BOOKS GIVEAWAY

2 FREE ROMANCE BOOKS!

2 FREE WHOLESOME ROMANCE BOOKS!

GET UP TO FOUR FREE BOOKS & TWO FREE GIFTS WORTH OVER $20!

We pay for everything!

YOU pick your books – WE pay for everything.

You get up to FOUR New Books and TWO Mystery Gifts...absolutely FREE

Dear Reader,

I am writing to announce the launch of a huge **FREE BOOK GIVEAWAY**... and to let you know that YOU are entitled to choose up to FOUR fantastic books that WE pay for.

Try Harlequin® Special Edition books featuring comfort and strength in the support of loved ones and enjoying the journey no matter what life throws your way.

Try **Harlequin® Heartwarming™ Larger-Print** books featuring uplifting stories where the bonds of friendship, family and community unite.

Or TRY BOTH!

In return, we ask just one favor: Would you please participate in our brief Reader Survey? We'd love to hear from you.

This FREE BOOKS GIVEAWAY means that we pay for everything! We'll even cover the shipping, and no purchase is necessary, now or later. So please return your survey today.

You'll get **Two Free Books** and **Two Mystery Gifts** from each series to try, altogether worth over **$20!**

Sincerely

Pam Powers

Pam Powers
For Harlequin Reader Service

FREE BOOKS GIVEAWAY
Reader Survey

1	2	3
Do you prefer stories with happy endings?	**Do you share your favorite books with friends?**	**Do you often choose to read instead of watching TV?**
○ YES ○ NO	○ YES ○ NO	○ YES ○ NO

YES! Please send me my Free Rewards, consisting of **2 Free Books from each series I select** and **Free Mystery Gifts**. I understand that I am under no obligation to buy anything, as explained on the back of this card.

❏ **Harlequin® Special Edition** (235/335 HDL GQ5J)
❏ **Harlequin® Heartwarming™ Larger-Print** (161/361 HDL GQ5J)
❏ **Try Both** (235/335 & 161/361 HDL GQ5U)

FIRST NAME

LAST NAME

ADDRESS

APT.#

CITY

STATE/PROV.

ZIP/POSTAL CODE

EMAIL ❏ Please check this box if you would like to receive newsletters and promotional emails from Harlequin Enterprises ULC and its affiliates. You can unsubscribe anytime.

BUSINESS REPLY MAIL

FIRST-CLASS MAIL   PERMIT NO. 717   BUFFALO, NY

POSTAGE WILL BE PAID BY ADDRESSEE

HARLEQUIN READER SERVICE
PO BOX 1341
BUFFALO NY 14240-8571

NO POSTAGE
NECESSARY
IF MAILED
IN THE
UNITED STATES

dress for dinner with Desmond, Shane and his girl-friend.

Maybe she wasn't as much of a homebody as she'd assumed. Maybe her quiet lifestyle was more about a lack of things to do. Something she should consider. Maybe when the summer was over and she moved back into her condo, she should think about expand-ing her social horizons. Maybe start taking a class or join a volunteer group. She'd been considering get-ting one of those foreign language apps to brush up on what she would guess was her very rusty college Italian. Instead of that, she could take a class at the community college and be with people.

After she finished applying her makeup, she added "check out Italian classes" to her calendar so she wouldn't forget, and then stepped into her dress.

It was the same one she'd worn to the Chihuly event, but it wasn't as if she had two "nice dinner" dresses. Her social events tended to be more casual. But when Shane had suggested dinner and named a restaurant, she knew that casual wasn't going to cut it.

As she pulled the hot rollers out of her hair, she wondered about the mystery date her brother would be bringing. He hadn't said much about her, beyond that he liked her. As she rarely met anyone he was dating, tonight was going to be fun.

She fluffed her hair, put in the pair of pearl earrings her parents had given her for her twenty-first birthday, then went downstairs.

Even though she was braced, she still had to consciously keep her mouth from falling open when she saw Desmond. The man could wear clothes. Once again he had on dark trousers and a dark shirt. Nothing overly special, yet he looked sexy and strong and more than a little tempting.

He smiled at her. "You look beautiful."

She waved away the compliment. "I know this is the dress I wore last weekend, but I wasn't prepared for all the fancy dinners and parties. My teacher's wardrobe isn't up to your level."

"You always look perfect."

She raised her eyebrows. "Perfect? Really? Don't you think that's pushing it just a little?"

"Not at all."

She sighed. "You are a great date. Do you know that, because you are." She shifted her wrap to her other arm. "I can't wait to meet Shane's girlfriend. He's been going out with her at least five weeks. Mom and I don't have the original start date of their relationship, so we can't be sure. Even if it's just five weeks, that's like a personal best for him. She's given me a list of questions to ask. I hope I can remember them all."

Desmond shook his head. "Does it occur to you

that conversations like this are one of the reasons your brother keeps his private life to himself?"

She grinned. "Of course, but who cares about him being uncomfortable? We need information!"

"You'll have a whole dinner to ask your questions."

"Oh, because you don't want to know anything? You have to be just as curious as I am."

Desmond glanced away, as if hiding something from her.

"What?" she demanded. "You know something. What is it? Tell me!"

He returned his attention to her. "Shane is my friend and anything he and I have discussed will stay between the two of us."

"That's so unfair. Not even a hint? Tell me something. You have to!"

He took her hand in his, brought it to his mouth and lightly kissed her knuckles. "As I said before, you look beautiful and I'm looking forward to spending the evening with you."

While she appreciated the compliment and the feel of his mouth on her skin, she knew he was trying to distract her from her interest in her brother's personal life.

"You're very loyal," she grumbled, snatching back her hand. "It's disappointing."

"I would be just as loyal to you."

An interesting concept, she thought. She suspected he was telling the truth. From what she'd observed, Desmond would be an excellent boyfriend. Attentive, kind, funny, charming.

"Rosemary was never good enough for you," she told him. "You should have listened to me."

"Yes, I should have. Shall we go?"

They drove to the restaurant where he handed off his car to the valet. Nissa looked around at the waterfront setting. Despite the fact that they were meeting at seven, it was plenty light. Sunset in this part of the country was still after eight thirty.

As they walked toward the entrance, Desmond put his hand on the small of her back. She instinctively moved closer to him, trying not to get too caught up in the heat from his touch. He was being polite, nothing more.

Once inside, he gave Shane's name and they were immediately shown back to a table by the water. Her brother was already there, and next to him was a petite, dark-haired woman. She was pretty, with an air of quiet elegance Nissa immediately liked.

They both came to their feet when she and Desmond approached the table. Shane engulfed her in a big bear hug before kissing her cheek.

"Hey, munchkin."

"Hey, yourself." She gazed into his eyes. "You good?"

His smile was happy. "I am." He turned. "Nissa, this is Coreen. Coreen, my baby sister, Nissa."

They shook hands, then Shane introduced Desmond. The four of them took seats across from each other. Nissa told herself not to stare but it was hard not to be interested in her brother's date. She couldn't remember the last one he'd introduced to anyone in the family. There had been Becky back in high school, but they'd known her for years before she and Shane had started going out.

"It's wonderful to finally meet you," Coreen told Nissa. "I've heard so much about you."

Nissa glanced suspiciously at her brother. "Is that good or bad?"

He grinned. "I only told her the good stuff. It didn't take long."

"Ha!" She pointedly turned away from him and looked at Coreen. "Shane said you're a doctor?"

"I am." Coreen smiled. "I'm an emergency room pediatrician at the hospital."

Nissa smiled at her brother. "Like I said before, Mom will be so proud."

"That's the least of it. I know she's going to grill you later."

"She won't have to grill me. I'm giving up everything I know for free." She smiled at Coreen. "Shane has been pretty quiet about you, so we're all curious. I'm here representing the entire family, but don't worry. We're a friendly bunch."

"That's what I've heard. Shane told me you're a teacher. That's a wonderful profession. You must have a lot of patience."

"So speaks the pediatrician."

"I like kids."

"Me, too."

Shane leaned toward Desmond. "They don't need us here for the conversation."

"Apparently not."

Nissa ignored them both. "I usually get a summer job but this year, for an assortment of reasons, I've been doing temp work. It's been interesting. I spent a couple of weeks at a doggie day care. That was fun, but made me want to have a dog. Then I delivered flowers for a few days. Now I'm working for some big international company that is doing a very large mailing. They've brought in people to stuff envelopes and apply postage. I keep reminding my boss about the existence of email, but so far she's not listening."

Their server appeared and they all ordered drinks, then discussed the menu. Coreen was pleasant and obviously crazy about Shane, which made Nissa like her more.

Coreen talked about how long she'd been at the hospital and how she'd moved up from Los Angeles where she'd done her residency at the UCLA Medical Center.

Nissa listened attentively, enjoying the information and how approachable Coreen seemed, only to be distracted by Desmond and Shane having some kind of silent communication. It wasn't anything overt—more subtle eye contact and a quick head shake on Desmond's part, as if he didn't want to do whatever Shane expected.

"I've only ever lived in the Pacific Northwest," Nissa admitted. "Born and raised. Our dad was a ferryboat captain for years. In the summer we would tag along on his trips." She looked at Desmond. "So his boat is way bigger than yours."

"Thank you for putting me in my place."

The server appeared with their drinks. Shane raised his glass.

"To finally getting together," he said.

"And meeting Coreen," Nissa added.

"Desmond and I met at boarding school," Shane said. "I was there on scholarship, but he got in the old-fashioned way. His parents paid the bill."

Nissa looked at her brother, trying to figure out why he would say such an odd thing.

"I was nervous about having him as my roommate," Shane continued. "But we got along right away. I used to drag him home with me every holiday so he didn't have to rattle around alone in his massive estate."

"I came willingly," Desmond said mildly enough, but there was something in his tone.

Nissa couldn't place it. Not annoyance or even resignation. Concern, maybe? Exasperation?

"We liked having him around," Nissa said, still confused about what was happening between the two men. "I had a huge crush on him when I was a teenager."

"I didn't notice," Desmond murmured.

Nissa laughed. "You knew about it, but of course you didn't do anything about it. Such a gentleman."

"How long have you two been going out?" Coreen asked.

"They're not dating," Shane said, his voice a little loud. "You thought they were together?" He laughed. "They're just friends. Have been for years. The crush thing is long over."

Okay, this was too strange, Nissa thought, unsure of what to do or say. She glanced at Desmond, but he was too busy watching Shane to notice her.

Not sure if she should say something or ask to speak to her brother alone, she decided to try changing the subject.

"Anyone know what's good here?" she asked, picking up her menu. "I would guess the seafood is delicious."

They each studied their menus. The server came by and told them about the specials, then took their orders. Conversation took a more conventional turn and Nissa started to relax enough to enjoy herself. But between the salads and the entrees, Shane surprised her by asking to speak with her outside.

"Family business," he said to Coreen and Desmond. "We won't be long."

Family business? What family business? Nissa followed him out onto the deck and turned on him.

"What has gotten into you? You're acting strange, even for you, and it's freaking me out. If you're this weird on your dates, it's no wonder you've never gotten married."

Instead of laughing at her or getting annoyed, Shane surprised her by apologizing.

"I should have warned you," he said. "About what was happening."

"I have no idea what you're talking about. You'd better tell me or I'm calling Mom."

Shane grinned. "That's your best threat? You'll call Mom?"

"You don't think she and Dad will get in the car and drive over the mountains to check on you?"

His humor faded. "Oh, right. They will. Okay, so none of this is about you. I'm testing Coreen."

"Testing her how? And why?"

He shuffled his feet, as if buying time. "Look, I like her."

"Yes, I can see that. For what it's worth, I like her, too. In a totally different way," Nissa added. "So what does that have to do with anything?"

He looked at her. "I don't like women."

Nissa laughed. "Since when?"

He groaned. "I mean, I don't get involved. I don't do serious. But with Coreen, I'm tempted to take things further and I want to make sure she's interested in the right things."

She poked him in the chest. "You're not making any sense."

"Desmond is a rich, good-looking guy. Coreen knows who he is and that he's single. Will she hit on him while we're gone? That's what he's going to let me know."

She felt her mouth drop open and had to consciously close it. "You're setting a trap for your date?"

"It's not a trap if nothing happens."

"And Desmond agreed?"

"He wasn't happy. He told me I was a jerk for doing this to her, but he said he would help me out."

Nissa had no idea what to say to that.

"But I like Coreen," she complained. "I don't want to find out she's icky and I don't want you to lose her because you're a moron."

"Better I find out now than in a year."

"Or you could just talk to her and ask the question."

"If she's who I hope she is, the question will break her heart. If she's not, she won't tell me the truth." He glanced at his watch. "They've had enough time. We can go back in."

"And say what? If she asks what we've been talking about, what should I say?"

"Tell her we were discussing Mom's birthday present."

"I'm not a good liar."

He put his arm around her. "One of your best qualities, Sis."

DESMOND

"You're quiet," Desmond said, thinking that it was better to simply state the obvious than to try to talk around it. "Are you angry?"

"About what Shane did to Coreen?" She looked at him. "No, but I am confused about why he felt he had to test her that way. I asked him why he didn't just ask what was going on with her and he pointed out that someone who would go after you wouldn't be honest with him, which I guess is right… But the whole situation makes me sad. Why isn't my brother more trusting of women?"

"You'll have to ask him that."

"Oh, like he'll tell me anything." She sighed. "Someone, somewhere really broke his heart."

"Yes."

She understood that was a big admission for him. As for the details, she would work on getting them from Shane.

"You weren't happy playing along," she said. "He told me you thought he was being a jerk."

"I was just hoping he was wrong to worry about Coreen. I don't want to have to tell my best friend that the woman he's dating just tried to pick me up."

"Is that an ongoing problem?"

He thought of the women who had been thrilled to be alone with him, regardless of who they were with. How they'd moved closer, running their hands along his arm or his thigh, offering their number and anything else he might want. They knew he was rich and for some people, money mattered more than anything.

"Sometimes. Not with your brother's dates."

"But Coreen was good, wasn't she? Tell me she didn't do anything, because I really like her."

"She wasn't the least bit interested in me. She talked about how great Shane is and how much she had wanted to meet you. I think she's the real deal."

"That makes me happy."

He smiled. "I thought it might."

"I'm just surprised. I just thought Shane had it all together, but he doesn't. Sure, he's a gifted surgeon and he has a great house and stuff, but inside, he's just as broken as everyone else."

She looked at him. "I know you didn't want to help him, but you did anyway. You're a good friend."

"I'd do anything for him."

"I know. You love each other." She smiled. "In a very manly, friendship kind of way."

Some of his tension faded. "We do."

He pulled into the garage and they both got out. When they walked into the kitchen, Nissa came to a stop and faced him.

"Do you miss Rosemary?" she asked.

Her eyes were the most perfect shade of blue, he thought, meeting her gaze. Clear and deep, with long lashes.

"No."

She smiled. "You don't want to elaborate?"

"She married me for my money and when I told her the marriage was over, she walked away. There wasn't much to miss."

"I told you not to marry her."

"Yes, you did, and next time you give me that kind of advice, I'm going to listen."

"Do you think it's going to work out with Coreen and Shane?"

"I hope so. She seems crazy about him. Any other questions?"

Like did she want him to come upstairs with her and make love all night? Because if she did, he was more than willing.

But instead of asking that, or teasing him or mentioning a snack, she simply said, "I'm tired and I'm going to bed. Good night, Desmond."

And with that, she was gone, leaving him alone with the sense of having blown something important. Not that he could, in any way, say what it was.

NISSA

Nissa kept to herself for the next few days. The dinner with her brother had unsettled her—no, not the dinner. The testing of a perfectly nice woman because Shane didn't want to trust her.

His need to do that surprised her, and made her wonder what else she didn't know about him and about Desmond. She felt foolish—like the country mouse seeing the big city for the first time, and it wasn't a happy view. She felt sad that Shane felt the need to go so far to protect himself, which meant something really bad had happened to him and she had no idea what.

The evening had also opened her eyes about what

Desmond's dating life must be like. How could he know if someone was in it for him or for the money?

Monday after work she drove back to his big house, determined to shake off her mood. If Shane wanted her to know the details of his personal life, he would have told her, so she was going to have to let that one go. As for Desmond, she could only be herself around him and draw comfort from the fact that he knew she liked him for him. The rest of it was just a part of who he was, but not important to her.

After showering and changing her clothes, she went downstairs and talked with Hilde about the progress being made on the decisions for the remodel. Construction was due to start in mid-September and would take about four weeks. She would be long gone by then, but promised to come back and view the finished kitchen.

She checked her email and social media, texted with Marisol, all the while listening for Desmond's car. When she finally heard him pull into the garage, she got up and walked through the kitchen to wait for him.

He stepped into the house and saw her. His immediate warm, welcoming smile made her feel all tingly down to her toes.

"I'm ready to talk," she told him. "Because I know you've been missing my sparkling conversation."

"I have. Let me put my things away and I'll join you in the family room."

She went to wait for him. He returned in about ten minutes. He'd changed out of his suit and looked casual and relaxed in jeans and a T-shirt.

"The young executive at home," she teased. "It's a good look."

"Thanks." He crossed to the bar and started pulling out ingredients. "Why are we speaking again? I ask the question out of curiosity and not to annoy you. I missed having you to talk to."

"I needed to work things out," she admitted. "The money thing is so strange to me. Although in Shane's case, it's not about money. I suppose that's what upset me as much as anything. Someone damaged him and I don't know who it was or when it happened."

"He was gone a lot," Desmond reminded her. "He went off to boarding school when he was thirteen, and then to college."

"Meaning there are many parts of my brother's life I don't know about?" She nodded. "I figured that part out. I was just surprised by all of it. And sad for both of you. It must be hard to be so afraid to trust someone you want to care about. I don't think I could do that." She smiled. "I do tend to just put it all out there."

"That's part of your charm."

"It's a different view of the world."

He held out a lemon drop for her and picked up his scotch.

"Don't stop trusting people," he said. "I've always admired how you embrace the world, flaws and all."

They took their usual seats on the facing sofas.

"You make me sound foolish."

"No." He looked at her, his gaze intense. "I said I admire you, Nissa, and I mean that."

He did? "You do?"

"Yes. You have the purest heart of anyone I know. I only want good things for you."

There was something in the way he spoke the words, as if there was a secret message in them. One she couldn't decipher.

He smiled. "I want you to marry for love."

"Why else would I get married? Giving someone your heart, accepting theirs in return, that's the point of marriage. Knowing that for the rest of your life, this is the one person you can count on to care about you, no matter what."

His dark gaze was steady. "Did you have that with James?"

"No, and that's why I didn't marry him. Something was missing. It took me a few months to figure that out, though. He kept pressing me to set a wedding date and I kept resisting. Then one day I knew what was wrong. I didn't love him enough to want to marry him."

"I'm sorry you had to go through that."

"Me, too. It was hard on both of us." She thought about how angry James had been when she'd ended things, but the fury had quickly turned to hurt. He'd told her he would love her forever. She hoped that wasn't true.

"Do you ever hear from him?" Desmond asked.

"No. I gave him back his ring and that was the end." She looked at him. "Do you hear from Rosemary?"

"No." He smiled. "Let us remember, she wasn't in the marriage for me. Once she realized she wasn't getting any money, she was ready to move on."

"That makes me sad."

"Why? Marrying her was a mistake, but a recoverable one."

"Yes, but she reinforced all your ideas about women only being after you for money. That's not right and it's not true. Not everyone is like that."

He surprised her by smiling. "That's true. Some of them are after me for the sex."

Despite the emotions churning inside of her, she laughed. "You are such a guy."

"Women like sex, too."

"They do," she admitted, thinking that she found him very sexy and that she'd enjoyed every fantasy she'd ever had about him. Based on what she knew about him as a man, it wasn't a giant leap to think about how he would be as a lover. He liked to see a job through—an excellent quality for a sexual partner. Not that they were going there.

"Life is complicated," she said, picking up her drink.

"It can be."

"I remind myself that a year from now, I'll be in Italy. That helps."

She caught a slight tightening around his mouth.

"What?" she demanded. "You were thinking something."

"I wish you didn't have to work at a job you don't like to pay for it."

She stared at him. "What are you talking about?"

"You hate stuffing envelopes."

"Of course I do. It's not the sort of thing anyone likes, but it's no big deal and totally worth it."

"If you'd just let me give you the money," he began.

She set down her glass and glared at him. "Stop, Desmond. We've talked about this. No and no. This is *my* trip and I'm happy earning the money. This is my dream and I want to make it happen. I want the satisfaction of having earned it. Why can't you understand that?"

"I do understand that you're being stubborn. We're friends. I care about you. Why won't you let me do this for you? Then you could take off the rest of the summer and enjoy yourself."

"Life doesn't work that way."

"Sometimes it does. Sometimes good things happen. If you let them. It makes me feel good to help you. Why is that bad? Why can't you accept that? Why do you always have to be so stubborn about everything?"

"What?" she said, her voice rising slightly. She wasn't mad—not yet—but she was on the road. "You're the one who totally expects to get his way. Why does it annoy you that I want to do the work? Most people have to."

"I agree and I wish I could change that, but I can't. However, I can give you a trip to Europe." He leaned toward her. "You're being ridiculous. If we were married, you'd have no trouble letting me pay for the trip or anything else. Why is this different?"

The absurdity of the statement propelled her to her feet. "You didn't just ask that. If we were married, we would have agreed to spend the rest of our lives together. It's totally different from being friends." She put her hands on her hips. "Not that it matters because we're never going to *be* married, or anything other than what we are, mostly because you're never going to ask me out. Heaven knows we're certainly never sleeping together. What if my brother disapproves? What if he tells you not to? So don't talk to me about—"

The reality of what she'd just said sank in slowly, but when it was fully absorbed, she stopped talking midsentence.

No, she thought in horror. *No. No. No.* She hadn't just said that. About them being married or more than they were or the sex thing. She couldn't have because if she had, Desmond would assume some or all of it was what she wanted. He would think she'd been hoping for more all this time, and then he would, well, she didn't know what, but it would be bad.

His dark gaze locked with hers. She saw questions in his eyes and tension in his body. She didn't know which was worse—the comment about marriage or the hint about sex. Were they equally bad or should she rank them somehow?

The silence between them lengthened. Nissa wasn't sure what to do. Running away seemed the most logical next step, but to where? Her room upstairs? Once she closed the door behind her, she was going to have to stay there forever, slowly starving to death. Once she was dead, she wouldn't care about facing him.

"Did you want me to ask you out?" he asked, coming to his feet.

She held in a high-pitched keening sound she

could feel building up inside of her chest. "Um, back in high school? After prom? Yes, I did. I called you and you never called me back."

"I meant now."

Crap. Double crap. Did he really expect her to answer that? To bluntly say what she thought of him and hoped would happen? Not that she'd ever put her hopes into words, but she was fairly clear on the fact that she—

"Nissa?"

She cleared her throat, careful to keep her gaze fixed on a point just over his shoulder. "You're very attractive and we have fun together. Going out would be, you know. Nice."

"So you like me."

She groaned as she returned her gaze to his. "Of course I like you. We've been friends for years. Why are you doing this? Why all the questions? Why don't you tell me how *you* feel? I get why you didn't ask me out back in high school. Shane was right. I was too young for you. But it hasn't been that way for a while and it seems to me if you were the least bit interested, you would have done something, so I don't get why you feel the need to drag all this information out of me when you have no intention of—"

He circled the coffee table and reached for her. One second she was feeling confused and embarrassed and the next she was in his arms and his mouth was on hers and she was remembering how glorious his kisses had been so many years ago and discovering they were just as delicious now.

Chapter Eight

NISSA

Desmond gave as much as he took, kissing Nissa with a need that fed her own desire. No matter how tightly he held her, she wanted to be closer. His hands stroked up and down her back, then dropped lower to cup her rear. She instinctively arched toward him and was both surprised and happy to feel the hard ridge of his erection against her stomach.

She pulled back and stared at him. "You want me!"

One corner of his mouth turned up. "Why are you surprised?"

"You're always so controlled. I believed you about

just being friends and you were lying the whole time."

"I wasn't lying. I was doing the right thing."

"And now?"

"You seem willing to go in another direction."

This conversation had more twists and turns than a round of Candyland, she thought. "So you want to sleep with me."

"That's more blunt than I would have put it, but yes. I would very much like to take you to my bed and make love with you."

The words sent heat pouring through every part of her. A faint tingling began to radiate out from her midsection. She felt her breasts getting heavy and a telltale ache settling low in her belly.

"That's very clear," she said quietly.

"Nothing has to happen," he told her. "I mean that. You're too important to me to want this relationship messed up. We can go back to what we've always been. I won't ever push you."

She believed him. Not only did she know his character, Desmond had never lied to her.

She thought about how much she liked him and how good they were together in every other way, then she put her hands on his chest.

"I'm on the pill but I don't have condoms with me. I'm hoping you do."

His eyes dilated. "Upstairs."

She smiled. "I've never seen your bedroom."

"Would you like to?"

"Very much."

They stared at each other for another two heart-beats, then he took her hand and led her toward the stairs. They went up faster and faster, until they were racing to the top.

Laughing together, they ran down the hall and into his bedroom. Nissa had a brief impression of high ceilings, a large fireplace and a view of the Sound before she saw the massive bed against the far wall. Then Desmond was kissing her and nothing else mattered.

While his lips claimed hers, his hands were everywhere. She understood his desire to touch all of her because she felt the same way about him. She stroked his back, his shoulders and his chest. He tried to pull off her T-shirt while she attempted to work the buttons on his shirt.

They bumped hands and arms and nothing was accomplished. Finally they stepped away from each other and quickly stripped off their clothes. Then they were holding each other, skin against skin. He retreated again, just long enough to fling back the covers from the bed, before lowering her down and joining her.

He explored every inch of her, with his hands and his tongue, teasing her into an arousal that had her panting as she strained toward her release. Kissing her deeply, his skilled fingers between her legs, he eased her over the edge, then drew out her orgasm until she was boneless.

Only then did he enter her, his dark eyes locked with hers. He filled her over and over again, exciting her until she had no choice but to soar a second time, with him only seconds behind.

NISSA

Satisfaction and happiness battled for dominance. Nissa, still naked and wrapped in Desmond's arms, her head on his shoulder, was willing to let them decide on the winner. She would be content with either or both emotions. Her breathing had returned to normal and her mind was starting to clear, but none of that changed the fact that she and Desmond had just made love.

She shifted so she could look at him. When his gaze met hers, he gave her a slow, sexy, "I'm the man" kind of look that told her he had zero regrets.

"That was nice," she murmured, her tone teasing.

"Very pleasant," he agreed.

They smiled at each other. He propped himself up on one elbow and stroked her bare shoulder.

"You're really all right?" he asked.

"Very."

"Good."

He moved his finger from her shoulder to her breast. Sparks immediately began to light inside of her. They got more intense when he reached her nipple and lightly stroked the tight peak.

"So next time, I was thinking you could be on top," he said, looking at her. "If that's all right."

"I can do that." Straddling him, arching into his thrusts. Yup, she was a firm yes.

He used his thumb and forefinger to gently pinch her nipple, before leaning close and taking it in his mouth and sucking. Pleasure shot through her, making a bee line for her core.

"That's really good," she breathed, her eyes sinking closed.

He got to his knees and shifted to her other breast, drawing it in and—

Somewhere in the distance she heard a high-pitched ringtone. At first she didn't recognize the insistent clanging noise, but then the meaning of it sank in and she pushed him away before scrambling out of his bed and diving for her shorts.

It took her two tries to answer, then she gasped. "It's happening?"

On the other end of the call, Marisol's voice was thick with tears. "They just called. They found a donor. Everything checks out and I'm scheduled for surgery tonight."

"I'm on my way." Nissa felt her throat tighten as she fought tears of her own. "I'm so happy for you. Tell the girls to hang tight. I know they're scared, but I'll be there for them and for you. Don't you worry."

"Thank you. I love you so much."

"I love you, too."

She hung up the phone and reached for the rest of her clothes. Desmond had gotten out of bed and crossed to her. She gave herself a second to admire his strong body before pulling on panties and picking up her bra.

"What's going on? Who was that?"

Because he didn't know. She'd told him Marisol was sick, but not the particulars.

She fastened her bra and pulled on her shorts. "Marisol has terminal kidney disease. We've been waiting for a donor kidney so she can have a transplant. One just came through." She pulled on her T-shirt. "I'm sorry the timing isn't the greatest, but I have to go be with the girls. Marisol is having surgery tonight so they need me. I hope you understand."

DESMOND

Desmond had no idea what Nissa was talking about. He'd known Marisol was ill, but it had been obvious that Nissa hadn't wanted to go into detail, so he'd never asked. A kidney transplant? Wasn't that a dangerous surgery? Of course if her disease was terminal, then not having the procedure wasn't an option.

All those thoughts were pushed aside when he realized Nissa was going to be leaving. He quickly pulled on his own clothes and followed her down the hall to her room. She darted into her closet and pulled out a small suitcase.

"My to-go bag," she said with a shrug. "Because I'll need to stay with the girls."

"I'll go with you."

She was already starting for the stairs. "You don't have to. I know this is sudden, but I have to get to her house and drive her to the hospital. I'll call. I promise."

He was on her heels. "I know you will, but that's not the point. You're dealing with a lot. I'll drive. My car will be more comfortable for Marisol and the girls. We can recline the front seat for her."

They'd reached the main floor. Nissa hesitated only a second before nodding.

"Thank you for the offer. I'll admit, my head is spinning."

They got into his car and he backed out of the garage. Once they were on the street, she gave him Marisol's address and told him the quickest way to get there.

"Tell me about Marisol's disease," he said quietly. "There's no other treatment?"

"No. Her doctors tried everything before deciding a transplant was her only hope of survival. Until then, she's kept alive by dialysis. I volunteered to be a living donor, but while our blood types would work—I'm considered a universal donor—we didn't pass the cross-matching test. Basically she has antibodies against my cells. You can only donate to other A or AB positive people."

"That's why you asked my blood type."

"I ask everyone," she said. "Just in case. I wanted to talk to her about doing a paired exchange. That's when you have a donor who is willing, but can't give to you. So you find someone else in the same position, but who can give to you. So far we haven't found anyone."

"You would have given her a kidney?"

A stupid question. It was obvious she would. Nissa loved her friend and she was simply that kind of person.

"Of course. She needs to live. She's got the twins and they've already lost their dad." Tears filled her eyes. She shook her head and inhaled. "I'm not crying. I'm not going to cry. I have to be strong for the girls."

"You'll be taking care of them," he said, starting

to understand what was happening. "You're going to what? Move into their house?"

"Yes." She turned to him. "I'm sorry, Desmond. I wanted to tell you all this before, but Marisol didn't want people to know. Things got weird when some of her friends realized she might die. Plus, she's protective of the girls."

"Are you their guardian?"

"If something happens to Marisol?" She nodded. "Yes. If she dies, I'll step in and raise them."

She spoke so calmly, he thought. As if she was simply going to water houseplants for a few weeks. But it wasn't that.

"What about your trip to Italy?"

He realized it was a ridiculous question as soon as he asked it, but couldn't call it back.

She smiled. "Marisol is going to be fine. That's what I believe. But if she's not, I guess I'll save a little longer and the three of us will go together in a few years. It's not like my dream trip is going away. Italy will still be there."

She was willing to turn her life upside down, he thought, stunned by her acceptance of such massive responsibility. He didn't know anyone else who would be willing to take on two children the way she was.

"Rylan and Lisandra must be terrified," he said.

"This is a lot for anyone to deal with but they're only ten."

"They've been very brave, but it is a burden. They don't like seeing their mom sick and I know they're scared about the possibility of losing her. They've both been in counseling, which helped." She shook her head. "I wish I could take her disease from her. I don't have the responsibilities she does. It would be easier for me."

His gut clenched at the thought of her facing death or transplant surgery, but he didn't say anything. Instead he focused on getting to Marisol's house as quickly and safely as he could.

When they arrived, Marisol was sitting on the sofa. She looked more pale than she had, but there was hope in her eyes. Her daughters were on either side of her, clinging to her. They had both been crying.

Nissa rushed over and knelt in front of the three of them, holding out her arms. "We're going to get through this," she said firmly, hugging them. "We're going to be strong and pray and come out the other side."

"You're a blessing," Marisol said.

Desmond felt out of place, and moved toward the small dining room to give them more privacy. He still couldn't completely absorb what was happening. Marisol was facing a terrifying procedure and there was nothing he could do to help. For once, his ability to write a check was meaningless. Not a feeling he enjoyed.

He circled the small table, part of him listening to the low rumble of voices in the other room, and part of him noting the battered table and rickety chairs. He moved into the kitchen and saw it was a decent size, but the cabinets needed replacing and the appliances were practically antiques.

"Desmond?" Nissa called.

He hurried back to the living room.

"We need to go," she said, standing.

The girls each picked up a tote bag, then Marisol struggled to get to her feet.

He immediately moved close and helped her up. "I can carry you to the car."

Marisol gave him a smile. "While that's the most action I've seen in years, how about you just help me walk there?"

"Whatever you want."

When they arrived at the hospital, someone was waiting with a wheelchair. Marisol had already preregistered so only had to sign a few forms before they took her upstairs. Nissa and the girls led the way to where they would wait out the surgery.

The waiting area was filled with comfortable sofas, a table and chairs and lots of books and board games. Nissa had brought blankets and pillows for when the twins were ready to try to sleep.

"They'll get to see Marisol before she goes into surgery," she said. "Just for a few minutes."

To say goodbye, he thought grimly. In case something went wrong. Because if Marisol died, Nissa would suddenly be both mother and father to two ten-year-old girls.

How had he not known that? Why hadn't she been talking about it, worrying and making plans? But she hadn't. She'd simply agreed to a life-changing possibility. Who did that?

A few minutes later, a nurse came and got them. Desmond stayed behind, wishing there was something he could do to help. The surgery was beyond him and Marisol already had a donor, but maybe something with the girls.

When the three of them returned, Rylan and Lisandra were both crying. Instinctively, he held out his arms and they surprised him by rushing to him and throwing themselves against him. He hung on tight.

"I know you're scared," he said. "But we need to think positive thoughts. Why don't we pray together, then decide what we want to do next? It's going to be a few hours until we hear anything."

"We're supposed to get an update every two

hours," Lisandra told him. "That's what the doctor said."

"Good to know."

Nissa sat next to him and the girls knelt on the carpet. They all joined hands and prayed for Marisol's safe recovery, then asked for blessings for the family of the person who had passed away, thereby donating the kidney for the transplant.

When they were done, Desmond watched while tears filled the girls' eyes and knew they were seconds from a very understandable meltdown. What they needed was a distraction.

"Is the plan for you to go live in Marisol's house?" he asked Nissa.

She nodded, looking a little shattered herself. "Yes."

"I have a suggestion. Why don't the twins come stay at my place while their mom is in the hospital?"

Both girls stared at him.

He smiled at them. "I have a very big house that might be fun for the two of you. You could each have your own room, but with a bathroom in between, so you're close."

Nissa brightened. "He's right. It's called a Jack and Jill bathroom. I'm not sure why. But it's very cool. Oh, and Desmond has a pool. And the house is right on the Sound."

The twins looked at each other, then at her. "You'll be there?" Rylan asked, her lower lip quivering.

"Of course. I've been staying there while my condo is rented out. It's very nice there. Hilde, the housekeeper, would love to spoil you both. She's a fabulous cook and she makes cookies and brownies."

He was glad Nissa was onboard with the idea. Everything had happened so quickly. Two hours ago, they'd been in his bed and now they were at the hospital, dealing with Marisol's surgery and her children.

The twins looked at each other and slowly nodded.

"That sounds nice," Lisandra said, wiping away tears. "But not until we know about Mom."

"Of course not," Desmond said quickly. "We're going to stay right here and wait to hear the good news."

Nissa shot him a grateful look, before pulling tablets out of the tote bags. "Okay, let's get comfortable and find something to entertain ourselves."

Time passed slowly. Two hours in, a nurse came and said the surgery was going as well as could be expected. Eventually the girls fell asleep on one of the sofas. Nissa rescued their tablets before they slid off onto the floor, then pulled him into a far corner of the room.

"Are you sure about all of us staying with you?"

she asked, searching his face as she spoke. "It's going to be a lot to take on."

He gave her a gentle smile. "Have you seen my house? There's plenty of room. Hilde will love it, and I think being somewhere else will be a distraction for the girls when they need one."

He waved his phone. "I've been doing some research on kidney transplants. After Marisol is out of the hospital, she's going to need to take it easy for a couple more weeks."

Nissa bit her lower lip. "She's going into a skilled nursing facility until she can come home."

"Or she could move into the house. There's a guest room downstairs and we can get a nurse in."

Her eyes widened. "Desmond, you can't do all that."

"Why not? I like Marisol and her kids. They've been through enough. You know the money doesn't matter to me." He chuckled. "I do like to write a check to solve problems."

"Don't say that. You're being so nice." She blinked several times as if holding back tears. "Having her come to your house would be wonderful, but it's a lot to take on."

He waved away the comment. "We'll have a nurse in to help. It will be easy. And she'll feel better knowing her daughters are right upstairs."

What he didn't say was that part of his motivation

was that he didn't want Nissa to move out. Not now. After last night, things were different between them. He wasn't sure what was happening, but he liked it. He wanted to keep her close for as long as possible.

"I'll talk to her in a few days, when she's feeling better," Nissa told him. "I'm sure she'll agree, but I can't say yes for her."

"Understood."

She shifted her weight. "About what happened earlier."

"You mean getting the call from Marisol?" he asked, pretending he didn't know what she was talking about.

"No, before-before. Us."

"Oh, that. Regrets?"

"No! Of course not." She blushed. "It was wonderful."

"Good. Me, too."

Her gaze locked with his. "I want to be with you again, but with the girls around, I can't. At least not at first. Because they're going to need me."

"I know. I thought that for the first couple of nights, they'd share a bed and you could sleep in the other room, so they could easily get to you if they need you."

"That's a great idea. I'll do that. Should I go back to the house and get the rooms ready?"

"I've already texted Hilde. She's taking care of it right now."

"You've thought of everything."

"I hope so." He drew her close and wrapped his arms around her. "We're going to get through this. Whatever happens, the girls have you and you have me."

"Thank you for understanding how important this is to me."

"Anytime."

He kissed the top of her head and released her. She returned to the sofa closest to where the girls slept. He would guess she was going to watch over them all night, if necessary. And he would watch over her.

NISSA

Marisol's surgery took four hours. The surgeon was pleased with the outcome and told them there hadn't been any complications. Now the real waiting game began. They had to get through the first twenty-four hours, then the second, and so on. With each passing day, she would get stronger.

The girls cried when they heard the news and fought leaving the hospital. Nissa knew they had been through so much—they had to be exhausted. She convinced them to get a little sleep at Desmond's house before they returned in the early afternoon.

They wouldn't be able to see their mom until after lunch sometime.

Despite the late hour, Hilde was there to greet them when they arrived at the house. She showed the girls their room and the adjoining bathroom. Nissa took Desmond's advice and suggested they share a bed, with her right next door. The twins were relieved by that idea and quickly got ready for bed.

Nissa stayed with them until they were asleep, then went into her own room where she found Desmond reading in the chair in the corner. He put down his book as she entered, then crossed to her and pulled her close.

As he held her tight, all her emotions seemed to crash in on her at once and she started to cry. Tears quickly changed to sobs that shook her body and made it impossible to get control. But he seemed unfazed, continuing to stroke her back and murmur quietly that she would be fine.

After several minutes, she managed to calm down enough to catch her breath and slow the flow of tears.

"I don't know what that was," she admitted. "I think I scared myself."

He smiled at her as he wiped her cheeks. "You've been dealing with a lot. It's good to get it out." He leaned in and lightly kissed her mouth. "I finally got Hilde to go home. She'll be back first thing to make breakfast. She can't decide between pancakes and waffles, so be prepared to have all the food on your plate."

Nissa managed a shaky smile. "She's been so wonderful."

"Having kids in the house is her dream. She's thrilled to have people to take care of."

He kissed her again, lingering just long enough to make her aware of the fact that about eight hours ago, she'd been naked in his bed. A situation she'd like to repeat—just not tonight.

As if reading her mind, he said, "Go to bed. You're exhausted. I'm right down the hall if you need me."

She looked into his dark eyes. "Thank you for everything. You've been amazing."

"I was happy to help."

With that, he walked out of the room.

She watched him go. She'd always known that Desmond was a great guy, but she hadn't known how dependable he was in a crisis. He'd calmly taken charge of the situation and had made everyone feel safe.

Funny how everything she learned about him only made her like him more and wonder what would have happened if he hadn't listened to her brother, all those years ago.

Chapter Nine

DESMOND

Desmond didn't get a lot of sleep that first night. He'd called to check on Marisol every hour. Her condition was unchanged, but the ICU nurse had said she was resting comfortably and her vitals were good. Now it was just a waiting game.

He got up early and showered, then headed downstairs. Hopefully the girls would sleep late. Getting some rest would make the stress easier to deal with. He'd told Hilde not to come until after eight, but of course his housekeeper was already at work in the kitchen.

When she saw him, she started to pour him coffee.

"So you don't listen to me anymore?" he asked, his voice friendly.

She smiled. "I want to be here when the girls wake up. To make breakfast and show them around the house. They need to feel safe here."

"Thank you."

"You're welcome."

He drank his coffee and chugged the protein drink Hilde made for him as he tried to decide if he should wait for Nissa to get up before heading to the office or instead write her a note. She made the decision for him by walking into the kitchen.

She looked pale, and there were shadows under her eyes. When she saw him, she crossed to him and wrapped her arms around his waist.

"I didn't sleep," she admitted, leaning against him. "I kept worrying and checking on the girls. But everything is good at the hospital and the girls slept through the night."

"I'm glad on both accounts."

She straightened and greeted Hilde, then walked over to the coffee. His housekeeper stared at him, her eyebrows raised. He stared back, not saying anything. Finally Hilde simply smiled and went back to work prepping for breakfast.

"What's the plan for today?" he asked. "Don't the girls have camp?"

"Yes, but they're going to stay home with me. We'll go to the hospital this afternoon. Seeing their mom is the best thing for them. She's already explained that she's going to look terrible, but that she'll be on the mend, so they're prepared."

Nissa grimaced. "As prepared as you can be, considering what's happening. I've already called in to work and told them I quit."

He stared at her. "Your job?"

"Uh-huh. I'm sure eventually the girls will want to go back to camp, but I'm not going to push them. I'll stay close. It's better for them."

"What about your Italy fund?"

She smiled. "It's doing okay, and if I have to put off my trip for a year, then I will. This is more important."

He knew enough not to (once again) offer to pay for everything. Although that argument had had a fairly stellar outcome. Still, the trip was important to her.

She took the cup of coffee Hilde handed her. "I thought it might be fun for the girls and me to go to their house and paint their bedroom. They're a little older now and the bright pink is getting to be a bit much."

He thought about the worn furniture in the living room and dining room and how the kitchen needed updating. The girls' room was probably in the same shape.

"Marisol's going to be in the hospital for ten or twelve days, then staying here for another couple of weeks. That's almost a month. Let's redo her house."

Nissa stared at him. "What are you talking about? Redo what?"

"All of it. Paint, refinish the floors, put new carpet in the bedrooms, fix up the kitchen."

"You can't do that."

"Why not?" He leaned against the island. "I give tens of thousands of dollars away every year to charities because I think it's important to help out where I can. Marisol has been to hell and back. Why can't I help her? I know her and I like her. Unless you think she'd be upset."

"I don't know what to think." She looked at him. "Just like that?"

"Wouldn't you do it if you could?"

"Sure. In a heartbeat." She sipped her coffee. "It would be a great project for the girls, but we'd have to come up with a kitchen design and what about contractors?"

"Desmond has people," Hilde said quickly. "I could help, too."

"You're outnumbered," Desmond said with a grin. "I'd like to do this for Marisol and her daughters. Let's give them their dream house."

"You're going to make me cry again," she said, turning away.

"Happy tears?"

She nodded. "Thank you, Desmond. I'm overwhelmed by your generosity. Yes, let's do it. Let's fix up Marisol's house."

NISSA

Three days after Marisol's surgery, Nissa stood in the middle of her friend's small house and stared at the petite woman with glasses. Erica was the architect Desmond had hired to take on the remodel. Nissa had told him they were just doing a remodel and no architect was required, but he'd only smiled at her and now she knew why.

"You want to what?" Nissa asked, trying to keep her voice from rising to a shriek. Lisandra and Rylan were staring at her with identical expressions of confusion, which made her feel better. At least she wasn't the only one wondering what on earth they were talking about.

"It's being done all over the neighborhood," Erica said with quiet confidence. "Adding a second story onto the house is time-consuming and expensive, but adding a second story to the garage is much easier. Many of these older houses are well constructed, with strong foundations that can take the weight. I've already confirmed that."

She unrolled large sheets of paper and put them on the kitchen table.

"This is only a two-bedroom house," Erica said, pointing to the drawing of the original floor plan. "With a single bathroom. The master is a decent size, which gives us a lot to work with."

She flipped to a second drawing. "We take the current full bath and make it an en suite with the master and take a little from the second bedroom to give Marisol a walk-in closet. The new staircase goes here, and we put a powder room under the stairs. A toilet and sink will fit just fine."

She smiled at the twins. "For you two, we take the whole space over the garage. You each get a large bedroom with a Jack and Jill bathroom. The toilet and tub-shower combo are shared, but you'll each have a sink with a long counter and plenty of storage. The closets are about the size you have now, but you'll each have one so that doubles what you're used to." She flipped to yet another page to show the upstairs.

"As for the kitchen," Erica continued, pointing to the room next to them. "The layout works great. I suggest we just do a quick update. New cabinets that go to the ceiling to provide more storage. New flooring and new appliances. Quartz countertops." She looked around. "Fresh paint throughout the house, and that's pretty much everything."

Nissa told herself fainting would cast a pall on an otherwise happy day, so she rested her hand on the back of a chair and did her best to keep breathing.

"How long would all this take?" she asked.

"Four weeks." Erica's voice was firm.

"That's not possible. Won't we need a permit, and won't that take a while?"

Desmond smiled. "I know a guy."

"Of course you do." Nissa turned to the girls. "This is a lot to take in. You'll want to think about it, but do you have any initial thoughts?"

The girls exchanged a look.

"We want to do this," Lisandra said firmly. "Mom's been talking about wanting to update the kitchen. She was saving for it before she got sick."

The girls disappeared into their mother's bedroom, then reappeared with a folder. Inside were pictures from magazines showing different kitchens.

"Excellent," Erica said. "This will give us a sense of her style. Oh, that's a beautiful farm sink." She pointed to a picture. "And I like these cabinets very much. They'll go perfectly."

Erica began rolling up her drawings. "I'll have a preliminary design to you by this afternoon. We'll meet tomorrow to choose finishes and the work will start the day after."

"So fast?" Nissa asked, barely able to breathe.

"Why wait?" Desmond looked at the girls. "We want to get this done, don't we?"

The twins nodded.

"It's like a TV show," Rylan added. "Where they do the work and later the family gets to see their new house!"

Erica smiled at the twins. "You two are going to have to think about paint color. We'll be putting in nice durable carpeting, so I'll have samples for you to look at tomorrow, along with fixtures for your bathroom. So you have homework."

Nissa's head was spinning. "We have to pick out bedroom sets."

"I'll have ideas for those, as well," Erica told her. "Not to worry. My office is going to be one-stop shopping."

The rich really did live different lives, Nissa thought. Not that she was going to complain. The house was going to be amazing and something that Marisol would have forever. But it was a lot to take in.

"All right," she said, going for cheerful, rather than panicked. "We're going to leave Erica to work her magic and go visit your mom. How does that sound?"

"Excellent," Lisandra said. Rylan nodded.

They thanked Erica for her help. Desmond said

he was going to stay with the architect to go over a few details and would meet her at home. As she and the girls walked to the car, the twins couldn't stop talking about the house remodel.

"I hope we can get storage under the bed," Lisandra said. "And lots of shelves."

"I want one of those bunk beds where the bottom bed is a full size and the top one is a twin bed so we can have sleepovers."

"Oh, that's a good idea. And we need desks." Lisandra waited while Nissa unlocked her car. "Mom needs a little desk in her room, too. Or maybe the cabinet kind so it can be closed up and look nice when she's not using it."

"We'll have to email Erica when we get back from the hospital." Nissa smiled at them. "Are you both going to be able to keep a secret?"

The girls nodded.

"Mom deserves a good surprise," Rylan said. "And so do we."

Later that night, Nissa read to the girls until they fell asleep. At first they'd complained they were too old to hear a bedtime story, but the ritual allowed them to relax and doze off.

Nissa made sure the bathroom night-light was on, then quietly left the room. As long as they were sharing a bed, she was in the room next door. She was sure that once Marisol was released from the hospital, the twins would feel better about everything.

She went downstairs and walked into Desmond's study. He was behind his desk, typing on his computer. As always, the sight of him made her heart beat a little faster. His appeal was more than how good-looking he was. She liked that he was strong, and being around him made her feel safe.

He looked up and saw her. His intimate smile did nothing to calm the fluttering.

"Are they asleep?" he asked.

She nodded. "They're exhausted. Between staying up most of the night of their mom's surgery and dealing with everything else, not to mention the excitement of the remodel, they were ready to crash."

"What about you?" he asked, coming to his feet.

"I'm a little tired."

"I bet."

He walked to the sofa in his office, grabbing her hand on the way. He sat and pulled her down next to him, then put his arm around her so she could rest her head on his shoulder.

He was warm and just the right height to be the perfect pillow, she thought, breathing in the scent of him.

"You smell good," she said, snuggling closer.

"So do you. How was your visit with Marisol?"

"Good. She's alert and feeling better every day.

The doctors are thrilled with her progress. She should be released right on time." She raised her head to look at him. "Is it still okay for her to come here?"

"Of course. I have a hospital bed and table being delivered on Monday. Marisol will have twenty-four-hour-a-day nursing care for the first few days, then a night nurse until she goes home. A physical therapist will be here to help her recover the muscle tone she will have lost by being in bed so much and Hilde has already consulted with the hospital's dietitian to get meal ideas."

"I'm impressed." She smiled. "I shouldn't be—this is how you roll—but I'm still impressed."

"How I roll?" His voice was teasing.

"You know what I mean."

He kissed the top of her head. "I do."

"The twins said they're ready to go back to camp," Nissa told him. "Tomorrow we have our meeting with Erica, but the day after, they'll return to camp."

"You sure they're ready?"

"I think they're the best judge of when that happens. I'm going to stay home so if they start to get upset and want to leave, I can go get them."

"You're a good friend."

"I love them."

"That's very clear," he said.

"You're being incredibly generous. Thank you for that."

"I'm happy to help, and you can stop thanking me. Helping Marisol and her family makes me happy."

"So you have a selfish motive," she teased.

"Very."

She laughed. "I know that's not true. You're a good guy, letting the girls stay here, and then taking care of Marisol when she gets out of the hospital."

"There's plenty of room in the house."

She sat up and slid back a little so she could see his face. "Why this house? It's huge and while it's beautiful, you buying it isn't intuitive."

"I wanted a home for a family."

"Sure, if you're going to have seventeen kids."

He chuckled. "I was thinking two or three, but I've always had a big house. I like the location and the size of the lot. The view. I felt comfortable here."

"You're right about that," she said. "The place is huge, but also homey." She cleared her throat. "Did Rosemary like it?"

One eyebrow rose. "Asking about the ex-wife?"

"Apparently."

He shook his head. "She didn't like anything about it. She didn't want me to relocate the company headquarters. She was happy there." He paused. "Some of it was Shane, I think."

"My brother? What does he have to do with anything?"

"She and Shane didn't get along. Neither of us

could figure out why, but his theory is that Rosemary was afraid Shane could see through to the real her."

"If he had been able to, he could have saved you a disastrous marriage. Or maybe not. Maybe you were determined to marry her. I warned you off her and you didn't listen."

"Something I still regret."

"Was the divorce difficult?"

"Not legally, but I felt as if I'd failed. My parents weren't happy, more because they wanted an heir than they cared about Rosemary."

Nissa remembered what Desmond's mother had said to her at the party and wondered if the other woman would be happy with anyone he chose.

"Rosemary tried to convince me not to give up on the marriage," he added. "When she figured out I was done, she stopped trying. She accused me of never loving her."

"That's not true. You married her. Of course you loved her."

"I didn't," he admitted. "I married her because she was what was expected. Love never entered into it."

Given what she knew about his parents and how his life was different from hers, she shouldn't be surprised, but she was.

"I'm sorry," she told him. "That makes me sad."

He touched her cheek. "I never want to make you sad."

"You're not responsible for how I feel." She deliberately lightened her tone to lighten the mood. "I hope you've learned your lesson, young man. Next time marry for love."

"Yes, ma'am."

Nissa studied him. "You gave her a generous settlement, even though you didn't have to, didn't you?"

"Why do you ask that?"

She smiled. "You so did. It's your style."

"I didn't want her to end up with nothing. The money didn't matter to me."

She again thought about what his mother had said at the party.

"I don't get marrying for money," she admitted. "Marriage is about love and connection and being together always. That's what I want—solid, steady love. I want kids and a dog and maybe a couple of cats and a regular life."

"Did you think you'd find that with James?"

The unexpected question made her wince. "No."

He stared at her. "I don't understand. You were engaged to him."

"I know." She shifted so she was sitting crosslegged, facing him. "Okay, I'll tell you but you have to swear to keep it to yourself."

"Who would I tell?"

"Shane. My mother."

"Ah, good point. You have my word."

She thought about the day James had proposed. "He and I were fighting. I had been complaining about your engagement to Rosemary because you wouldn't listen to me. James was frustrated. He said I talked about you all the time and if he didn't know better, he would think that I…"

Was in love with you. That was what James had claimed but Nissa wasn't comfortable blurting that out, so she searched for a slightly less embarrassing description.

"He felt I was too involved in your engagement," she amended. "He wanted to know if he mattered at all. I said of course he did. He wanted me to prove it. Then he asked me to marry him."

Desmond frowned. "That's not exactly romantic."

"It wasn't and now, looking back, I can see that even then I wasn't sure if I loved him the right way. I mean I loved him, but not enough to want to spend the rest of my life with him."

At Desmond's look of confusion, she added, "My mom walked in right then. She'd heard him propose and had assumed I said yes. She was thrilled and immediately told my dad and then it was kind of a done deal."

"You never said yes."

"Technically, I didn't. The next day he showed up with a ring and we were engaged."

"But you didn't get married."

"I kept putting off setting a date." For an entire two years, she thought, feeling guilty about how she'd handled the situation. "I told him I wanted to save the down payment for my condo first. He wanted to know why I was so determined to buy a place on my own instead of saving for a place for the two of us."

His dark eyes gave nothing away. "What did you tell him?"

"I didn't have a very good explanation. Eventually he got tired of waiting for me. He said I either had to pick a date for the wedding or the engagement was off. I gave him back the ring."

"He was a fool," Desmond told her. "He should never have let you go."

"I'm not sure keeping me was an option."

"I'm sorry for my part in it."

She touched his arm. "Don't be. If we hadn't been fighting over you, we would have been fighting over something else. We weren't right for each other. I just wish he'd understood that. I'm afraid I hurt him."

"You're too softhearted."

"That's not possible."

She was going to say more, but just then he leaned over and kissed her. The feel of his mouth on hers had her shifting toward him. He pulled her onto his lap and deepened the kiss. Heat immediately burst to life, making her tingly all over. She wrapped her arms around his neck and kissed him back, enjoying the feel of his tongue against hers and his strong hands moving up and down her back.

When he drew back, she was breathless and hungry.

"I know you can't stay the night," he began. "But maybe you could spare an hour."

Anticipation made her smile. "An hour is very doable."

Chapter Ten

DESMOND

The remodel of Marisol's house moved forward relatively smoothly. Desmond received daily updates from Erica, letting him know that the team was sticking to the aggressive schedule. He'd been forced to pay a premium for some of the work to be done so quickly, but the extra money was worth it. He wanted the house done on time.

Late Saturday morning, he took the girls out to see the progress. Nissa was working with Erica, picking out light fixtures and door pulls. While the twins were excited to talk about paint colors and bedding, they lost interest when it came to the details. He'd offered to keep them busy for a few hours. Nissa had looked doubtful but had agreed.

They arrived at the house to find workmen swarming all over the place. The second story was already framed and the new roof was nearly finished.

"Good thing it's not raining," Lisandra said as she scrambled out of his car.

"Summer's the best time to replace a roof," he agreed, making sure Rylan made it safely to the sidewalk. They walked in through the open front door and found themselves in the middle of a huge open space.

The kitchen had been gutted and the flooring had been pulled up. All the draperies were gone and shiny new windows replaced the old ones. Several patches covered the walls.

They made their way to the rear of the house. The master was empty, the windows were new and the carpet had been torn up. They could see the framing for the new closet and half bath under the stairs.

"It looks so different," Rylan breathed. "Mom's gonna love it."

They admired the kitchen cabinets stacked together in the center of the garage. Behind them were the new appliances. While the front yard was untouched, the backyard had been torn up. New sprinklers were being installed and most of the old, tired plants had been ripped out. Desmond knew that next week a new covered deck would be installed.

"This is really nice," Lisandra told him. "Thank you for being our fairy godfather."

He chuckled. "You're welcome."

"Can we get our hair cut?" Rylan asked. "It's long enough. We measured."

Desmond held up both hands. "No way. I'm not allowing you to cut your hair while your mom's in the hospital."

"Can we go to the mall?" Lisandra asked. "And then out to lunch?"

He eyed them suspiciously. "You're playing me, aren't you?"

The twins grinned at him, then each took one of his hands.

"It will be fun," Lisandra promised. "We can go to the Lego store. Boys like that."

"I haven't been to the Lego store before," he admitted. "I would like that."

An hour later, they were at the mall. The place was crowded with Saturday shoppers, but the girls stayed close. As promised, they took him to the Lego store where each of them chose something to put together. He promised to help with any of the tough parts, but suspected they would do fine on their own.

They went to the Cheesecake Factory for lunch. The twins sat across from him in their booth, each of them studying the very impressive menu. Once their orders were placed, they turned their attention back to him.

"When are we going to tell Mom about the house?" Rylan asked.

"I don't know. When do you think we should?"

The girls considered the question.

"We should wait until the very end," Lisandra said firmly. "So it's a super big surprise. Like on TV. So we shouldn't say anything now."

He looked at Rylan. "Do you agree?"

"Yes, but it's hard not to tell her when she asks what we've been doing. Plus I know the house is going to make her really happy."

"I hope it makes you happy, too."

The girls looked at each other.

"It will," Lisandra said. "We love our new rooms. They're so big and they're going to be beautiful and we can have friends over and everything. Plus the new kitchen. We can make cookies and help with dinner."

He didn't mention that Erica was replacing their mismatched cookware and dishes with new.

"I'm ready to go home," Rylan said quietly, then looked at him. "Does that make you mad? Your house is nice, but we miss our mom."

"It doesn't make me mad, at all. You've been

through a lot. First waiting for her to get a transplant, then the surgery itself. That's a lot to deal with."

Their server came and took their orders. When she'd left, Desmond smiled at them.

"I have liked getting to know you both. You've been really brave and strong."

"Mom told us we had to be," Lisandra admitted. "Sometimes it's hard. But Nissa's always there and now you're part of the family, too."

Rylan nodded. "It's like having a dad, only different." She brightened. "Like a stepdad."

The unexpected turn in the conversation made him uncomfortable. He'd never been good with people thanking him and hearing he was a part of the family was so much worse. Not that he didn't want to be—he liked the twins and enjoyed having them around. It was more that he wasn't sure he was up to the responsibility. What if he let them down?

"Are you Nissa's boyfriend?" Rylan asked.

"I, ah…"

Lisandra leaned toward him, her long hair swinging across the table. "Mom needs a boyfriend, so if you know any good ones, you should tell her."

Desmond did his best not to bolt for the exit. "You want your mom to start dating?"

The twins nodded. "It's time," Rylan told him. "We still miss our dad and we'll always love him, but our mom needs someone in her life. Someone who will love her and bring her flowers and make us all feel safe."

He was in over his head, he thought grimly, not sure what to say. Asking for a moment to text Nissa for help seemed inappropriate.

"You don't feel safe now?" he asked instead.

The twins exchanged a glance.

"We do," Lisandra told him. "Most of the time. Not while Mommy was sick, though. That was hard. We cried a lot. Now she's getting better so we can think about other stuff, like a stepdad."

Why him? Why couldn't they talk to Nissa about this? Or their camp counselor?

"Your mom might not be ready to start dating," he said with a shrug. "Hearts are tricky things. With being sick and then having the surgery, she's probably not ready to think about getting a boyfriend right this second."

"That makes sense," Rylan said. "But if you see a good one, you'll tell us?"

"I will."

He would also be letting Nissa know about the conversation so she could tell him if he'd screwed up anywhere and she had to step in and repair the damage. He liked the girls a lot—they were brave and smart and funny. But taking them on full-time? He couldn't imagine it. Yet Nissa had been willing to do just that. If Marisol hadn't pulled through the surgery, Nissa would be their legal guardian. He had no idea how she was so brave. He couldn't have done it, not for anyone. Kids needed so much, including someone who could love them back. And that person wasn't him.

NISSA

Nissa tried not to bounce in the front seat of Desmond's car, despite her growing excitement.

"I can't believe they're releasing her today," she said. "I knew it was going to be this week, but it's a day earlier than we'd thought. She's got to be so happy to be taking the next step of getting out of the hospital."

She looked at him. "Thank you again for letting her stay with you and arranging everything."

"Happy to help."

They'd gotten a call the previous evening from one of the nurses on Marisol's team. She was progressing so well, they were ready to release her, assuming things were ready at home. Nissa knew that the hospital bed and table were in place, along with a comfortable recliner.

She'd confirmed that he was good with the earlier date, then had let the nurse know they were ready to welcome Marisol home.

"Did we do the right thing with the girls?" she

asked anxiously. They'd made the decision not to tell them what was happening. Just in case something went wrong and Marisol had to go back to the hospital.

"They'll find out when they get home," he said easily. "Let them have the fun day at camp. There will be plenty of happiness to go around tonight."

"You're right." She leaned back against the seat. "My stomach is fluttering."

"You're a good friend."

"So are you. This isn't what you signed up for when you agreed to let me stay with you for a couple of months. Desmond, are you all right with the invasion? First me, then the twins, now Marisol and her nurses. There will be a physical therapist in and out, and my parents are planning to show up in a couple of weeks. It's too much."

He glanced at her. "Do you hear me complaining?"

"No, but—"

"Let it go. The house is happy with everyone running around and so am I."

"I want to believe you."

"Then you should."

He parked in the hospital lot.

"Once we know she's ready, I'll pull around front," he said.

Nissa nodded and got out.

"Let's go get Marisol so she can get started on the rest of her life."

Most of her transplant team showed up to say goodbye. Marisol hugged everyone, then waved as she was wheeled to the elevator. Nissa stayed close.

"Both your nurses have been in touch with the team," Nissa told her. "They understand where you are in your recovery and what the medication regimen is going to be. Once you're feeling better, we'll cut back on the nursing hours, but there's no rush on that."

Marisol grabbed her hand. "You're a good friend and I love you."

"I love you, too."

They left the elevator and moved toward the wide glass doors. Nissa could see Desmond was already in place, the car parked and the doors open.

As they went outside, Marisol raised her face toward the sun and took a deep breath. "This feels good," she said with a smile. "I'm a blessed woman."

Despite the recent surgery and her time in the hospital, she looked good. Her color was coming back and the faint gray cast to her skin had faded, along with the dark circles under her eyes. She was starting to look healthy again.

The drive home was uneventful. Marisol couldn't believe her beautiful room with the view of the Sound and a private patio. There were comfy chairs for her to rest in and the stone deck was smooth enough that she could use her wheelchair if she wanted.

"My goal is to get up and around as quickly as possible," she said. "I'm looking forward to my physical therapy. It's the only way to get strong again. I need to be in fighting shape to start my life!"

"We'll get you there."

Nissa and Marisol's nurse got her settled in bed. Nissa unpacked all her things, then sat in the chair next to her bed.

"The girls are going to totally freak when they find out you're here."

Marisol grabbed her hand. "Thank you so much for taking care of them."

"Of course. I was happy to step in while you had your little miracle."

Marisol yawned. "Sadly a car ride is too much excitement for me, but later, I want to talk to you. How are things with you and Desmond? Was he okay having the girls around? Anything going on that I should know about?"

Nissa thought about how she and Desmond were now much more intimate than they had been and the giant remodel waiting for Marisol, but kept quiet about it all. Her friend needed to rest.

"There's really not that much to share, but we'll definitely talk later." She kissed her cheek. "I promise."

"Good." Marisol released her hand and closed her

eyes, then immediately opened them again. "Go back to work. I know you quit to take care of the girls. I'm here now, so you can go get another temporary job to help with your Italy fund."

Nissa hesitated. "I'm not sure I should."

"You absolutely need to. I already feel guilty about the time you've spent with them when you could have been earning money. Believe me, if I had any extra money, I would insist you take it."

"Marisol, no! I'd never accept it. You're my friend. I love you and the girls and I'm honored to have been able to help. You have to believe me."

"I'll believe you when you go back to work, then."

"You're kind of bossy."

"You know it."

Nissa smiled and rose to her feet. "I'll call the temp agency right now."

"Good." Marisol closed her eyes. "See you in a bit."

"Yes, you will."

NISSA

Thirty minutes into her shift, Nissa knew she'd made a horrible mistake. Sign dancing was way harder than it looked. Her arms ached and her back wasn't happy, but the worst part of her job was the unsolicited advice people yelled as they drove by.

Apparently a large percentage of drivers felt she lacked rhythm, which was kind of insulting.

She'd thought the job would be easy—it was over a four-hour shift and the pay was decent. She'd watched several videos online to get an idea of how to twirl, dip and spin the sign. Again, it looked soooo much easier than it actually was.

Part of the problem was she kind of did lack the whole rhythm thing, and she wasn't much of a dancer. The big chicken tail she had to wear didn't help, either. It kept messing with her balance.

A pickup truck slowed and the driver's window rolled down.

"You gotta work it, lady. Put some heart into it."

The driver continued through the intersection.

She supposed being told to put some heart into it was better than other, less civilized comments she'd heard. Thank goodness she only had a half hour left on her shift. Once she got home and her body stopped hurting, she was going to have to reconsider her employment options. She was starting to think she wasn't sign-dancing material.

She tried to focus on the upbeat music playing in her earbuds, but it wasn't enough to distract her from the horn honks and the searing pain in her shoulders and upper arms. No one had warned her that the sign got really heavy in hour three. Obviously she was in much worse shape than she'd realized. She should take advantage of living in Desmond's house and use the gym there. Hadn't he mentioned it was in the basement somewhere? And while she wasn't a fan of basements in general, she had a feeling his was much less creepy than most.

"Nissa?"

She turned toward the sound of her name and saw a dark blue sedan pulling up to her corner.

"Nissa, is that you?"

She lowered the sign and walked toward the car, only to come to a stop when she saw James step out onto the sidewalk.

No, she thought, fighting humiliation. No, no, no! She was not just about to come face-to-face with her former fiancé while she was sign dancing and wearing a chicken tail.

He, of course, looked perfectly normal in suit pants and a white shirt with a blue tie. The sleeves were rolled up to his elbows—always a good look on a guy.

James was tall and handsome, with soft brown hair that was forever falling onto his forehead, and glasses that made him look smart and kind.

He moved toward her, smiling. "What are you doing?"

She held up the sign. "Working one of my crazy summer jobs."

"As a sign dancer?"

"I just started today." She rotated her free arm, feeling the pain shooting into her back. "It might not have been my best decision, but I'm—"

"Saving for something," he said, finishing her sentence. "Of course you are. You're the best saver I know." He studied her. "How are you? You look good."

"So do you."

He did. Not in any way that tempted her, but he seemed…happy.

She smiled. "Of course you're lacking a chicken tail, so obviously I look better."

He grinned. "Yeah, that tail is really something. How are you doing?"

"Good. On summer break, so that's fun, although I'm missing my kids. I've started counting down to the start of school. Oh, Marisol has a new kidney. She got a donor a couple of weeks ago and came through the surgery great. She's home recovering right now."

She and James had been together when she'd found out about her friend's illness.

"That's great news. I'm glad for her. How are the girls?"

"Excellent. They've been so brave. They're ten now."

"No, really? They're growing up fast."

They stared at each other. Nissa wondered how

they'd reached the awkward part of the conversation so quickly. At one point she and James had been planning their lives together.

"What's new with you?" she asked.

His expression turned sheepish. "I'm engaged."

"What? You are? That's amazing. Who is she? When's the wedding?" She dropped the sign, flung herself at him and hugged him. "James, I'm so happy for you."

He hugged her. "I'm happy for me, too. Her name is Cami and she's an office manager for a doctor. She's beautiful and funny and sweet and I'm crazy about her." He stepped back. "You were right about us, Nissa. When you said we weren't in love enough. I fought you on that, but you were right."

He shrugged. "What happened with you and me was kind of driven by circumstances. I always felt Desmond was between us in a way. Like he had a piece of your heart that no one else could touch. I wanted all of you."

"I'm sorry you felt that way," she said, careful not to say it wasn't true. Because sometimes she thought the same thing. That Desmond had always had a piece of her heart, and if that was true, she wasn't sure what it said about her future happiness with someone else.

"I shouldn't have proposed the way I did," he continued. "And I shouldn't have just gone along with everything when your mom overheard it. You never wanted to marry me."

"I'm sorry, James."

His smile returned. "I'm not. Because of what happened, I found Cami. It's what you talked about. The rightness of it. She and I get along much better than you and I ever did. And when she walks in the room, I know I'm the luckiest man alive."

Envy collected in her belly, but she ignored it. She was determined to be the kind of person she should be rather than pouting like a spoiled brat because James had found his one true love and she hadn't.

"Good for you," she said. "I'm so happy for you."

"Me, too. You seeing anyone?"

"No," she said, thinking she wasn't sure what she and Desmond were doing but traditional dating in no way described it. "Things are kind of crazy right now."

"You'll get there," James said kindly. "I know you will."

He reached for her again, hugging her. She returned the embrace, delighted for him and the knowledge that she didn't have to feel guilty about their relationship anymore.

Still hanging on to him, she drew back enough to see his face.

"So when's the big day? Tell me everything."

DESMOND

Desmond stared at Nissa as she smiled at James. Even from across the intersection, he could feel their connection. He'd left work to come by, not liking the idea of her dancing on a street corner. Not that he was checking up on her so much as making sure she was all right. But instead of finding her dancing around and shaking her chicken tail, he'd discovered her talking to James, of all people. Worse, she'd been hugging James, and he didn't know what the hell that meant.

The light turned green and he drove through, trying not to watch as Nissa laughed at something James said. Desmond returned to his office, planning to get buried in work, but once he got to his desk, he found he couldn't concentrate—not the way he should. Every time he looked at his computer he saw Nissa with James.

He stood and crossed to the window, staring unseeingly at the blue water of the Sound. In the distance were the San Juan islands, with Whidbey and Blackberry Islands the closest. Normally the view got his attention, but not today. All he could see was Nissa smiling up at James.

What had happened? Was it a chance encounter or were they really seeing each other? And if it was the latter, when had they gotten involved in the first place?

His phone buzzed. He walked over to his desk and saw the text was from Shane.

Sorry, man. Should have warned you earlier, but I didn't know things had changed until this morning. Hope you can handle it.

He swore silently. Shane knew? Things were serious enough that Shane knew? How had that happened? She'd told her brother about getting back together with James.

No, Desmond told himself. She wouldn't do that, not without saying something. He and Nissa were sleeping together. Okay, they'd never discussed their relationship or any expectations. Their transition from friends to lovers had been unexpected, and then Marisol's surgery and the arrival of the twins had kept them from talking, but he knew Nissa. She wasn't the kind of person who was involved in more than one relationship at a time.

Except he'd seen her with James himself. He knew that part of it was real. And Shane knew about it, so it was more than his imagination.

He dropped the phone onto his desk and collapsed in his chair. There was only one solution. When he got home, he was going to insist he and Nissa talk.

There was no way he was going to waste time speculating on the situation when he didn't have all the facts. It was the logical solution. Until then he would get his mind back on his job.

Which, as it turned out, was much easier said than done.

Chapter Eleven

NISSA

Nissa didn't consider herself a quitter, but when she returned to the office, she turned in her sign and chicken tail for good. She simply wasn't sign-dancer material. As she made her way to her car, she wondered how long her back and shoulders were going to ache. She'd always assumed her active lifestyle was good enough in the exercise department, but obviously not. She was going to have to start some kind of regular workout. Maybe a little jogging and certainly lifting weights. Her upper body strength was pathetic. And while she was at it, maybe she should look for a dance class. The world at large had not appreciated her moves.

She drove to Desmond's house, working on her plan, but as she pulled into the driveway, all thoughts of exercise and everything else fled when she saw a familiar silver Ford Explorer parked by the garage. She barely turned off her engine before grabbing her purse and flying into the house.

"Mom? Dad? You're here?"

"In the family room," her mother called.

Nissa raced into the large room and saw her parents sitting on a sofa, Marisol across from them looking happy, with good color and an easy smile.

"Look who turned up this morning," Marisol said with a laugh.

Roberta, Nissa's mother, stood and held open her arms. "I know, I know. We weren't supposed to be here for two weeks, but when you told me Marisol was out of the hospital, I said to your father that I just couldn't wait that long to see her and know she was healing."

Her mother hugged her and kissed her cheek. "Plus, we miss you, little girl."

Nissa laughed. "I think Marisol is the real draw, but I'm glad to have you here." She hugged her father. "Does Desmond know you've arrived?"

"Shane said he would text him." Roberta smiled. "That poor man is going to feel invaded."

"There are plenty of bedrooms," Nissa said, squeezing Marisol's shoulder. "The girls are going to be thrilled."

"They are," Marisol agreed. "They should be home from camp any second."

"I'm going to run upstairs and shower," Nissa said. "Don't go anywhere. I want to hear everything that's been going on."

Barry, her father, gave a mock sigh. "You two talk almost every day. How much could you have to share that the other doesn't know?"

"You know it doesn't work that way, Dad," Nissa told him with a grin.

She walked into the kitchen and found Hilde prepping for dinner.

"Your parents are so nice," the housekeeper said when she saw Nissa. "I knew they would be. Your mother said Shane and his girlfriend will be joining everyone for dinner."

Nissa winced. "That's a lot for you to get ready. Let me go take my shower, then I'll come back and help."

Hilde shook her head. "It's an easy menu and I'm happy to do the work. Desmond is alone too much. It's good to have the house full of love."

"I agree," Nissa said, before heading upstairs.

She made quick work of her shower, then blew out her hair and put on crop pants and a sleeveless shirt.

Her shoulders and back were still sore, but hopefully that would get better in the next couple of days.

She went back downstairs, hoping Desmond would be home soon. She wanted to see him. Not that there would be any sneaking around tonight, what with her parents just down the hall. Still, she always felt better when he was nearby.

She could hear conversation from the family room. The happy squeals told her the twins were back from camp. They'd always loved Nissa's parents, who acted as surrogate grandparents to the girls.

She'd just started for the family room when she heard the garage door open. She hurried to the mudroom where she waited until Desmond walked into the house. She rushed to him.

"Shane told you, right? You're not totally shocked my parents are here, right? They came early because of Marisol. They wanted to know she was all right. But this really makes for a houseful. Is that okay?"

Instead of smiling at her and reassuring her, he gave her a quizzical expression. "I saw the Explorer so I knew they'd arrived, but Shane didn't tell…" He frowned. "He texted me earlier."

"That's what my mom said. He warned you they were here."

Desmond's mouth tightened. "That wasn't exactly

what he said. I thought he was talking about something else."

She studied him, aware of a tension in his body. "What's wrong?" she asked. "There's something. Did you have a bad day at work?"

Before he could answer, her mother joined them.

"Desmond, there you are. I hope you're not too upset that Barry and I have rudely shown up with no warning."

He smiled at her as he hugged her. "Roberta, you're always welcome here. You know that."

"Thank you for saying that, even if you don't mean it." Her mother laughed. "We just couldn't stand to wait to see Marisol. She looks amazing. So much better than anytime in the past couple of years. The surgery was a blessing. I'm praying for the other family, who lost their loved one. Praying they'll find comfort in the organ donation."

She linked arms with him. "Now come join us, Desmond. We've taken over your family room. The twins are telling us about their day and Barry is going on about the Mariners. You know how that man loves his sports."

"I do."

Nissa trailed after them, hoping she was wrong about Desmond. But even as he chuckled and joined in the conversation, she couldn't help thinking there was something lurking in his eyes. Something she couldn't quite define, but knew in her gut the source wasn't anything happy.

DESMOND

Desmond escaped from the group in the family room long enough to go upstairs and change his clothes. In the few minutes he had to himself, he tried to figure out what was going on. Obviously Shane's text hadn't been about James at all, but had instead been a heads-up about Roberta and Barry showing up a couple of weeks early.

Based on his brief conversation with Hilde, he knew that Shane had also warned her, so another guest room was ready and his housekeeper was hard at work on dinner.

More pressing for him was the question about James and Nissa. Obviously Shane didn't know about them, assuming there was a them. Once again he knew he had to talk to her to get clarity on the situation, but given the crowded house, he wasn't sure how that was going to happen.

He went downstairs in time to answer the doorbell. Shane and Coreen stood on the wide porch. Shane grinned, but Coreen looked a little apprehensive.

"You got my text?" Shane asked. "I wanted to let you know you were being invaded."

"I did. And having your parents here isn't a problem."

"You say that now, dude," Shane teased. "Wait until they decide they never want to leave."

"I'd be okay with that."

He liked Roberta and Barry and in the past couple of weeks, he'd discovered he liked having people in his house. Nissa, most of all, but everyone else was welcome, too. After years of solitude, he enjoyed the conversation, the shrieks of the girls playing.

He greeted Coreen, then said, "There are a lot of people. The good news is you won't be the center of attention."

Coreen shot him a grateful look. "Thanks for saying that. I hope it's true."

Shane pulled her close and kissed the top of her head. "She can be shy. What can I say? She's charming."

As they walked toward the family room, Shane released Coreen. "You'll want to stay out of the line of fire for the next few minutes," he said quickly, before raising his voice and calling, "Do I hear my best girls?"

There was a heartbeat of silence followed by yells of, "Uncle Shane? Is that you?"

The twins raced into the foyer and flung themselves at him. Shane managed to pull them both up into his arms and squeezed them tight while giving them kisses on the cheek.

"You're so big! When did you get so big? How old are you now? Five?"

"Uncle Shane, you know we're ten," Lisandra said with a laugh.

"One day we're going to be too big to pick up and then what?" Rylan asked.

"You'll always be my best girls."

They all walked into the family room. While Shane introduced Coreen to his parents, Desmond pulled one of the sofas back a little so he could drag in a few club chairs scattered around the room. Nissa helped, tugging a small side table close.

"If you keep having this much company, you're going to have to reconfigure your family room," she teased, smiling at him.

Her expression was open and affectionate. There wasn't any guilt, no hint of her keeping secrets. But the knot in his gut said he still wasn't sure about what he'd seen.

"Who wants a drink?" he asked when there was comfortable seating for everyone.

"Do we get something fun?" Rylan asked.

Nissa headed for the kitchen. "I'm sure we can find something good for you." She glanced at Desmond. "I'll have whatever you make for my mom and Coreen."

He poured scotch for Shane and got a beer for Barry, then got out vodka, cranberry juice and the lavender simple syrup Hilde had left in the small bar refrigerator.

Nissa returned with glasses of watermelon lemonade for the girls.

"Dinner is going to be spectacular," she announced, handing the girls their drinks. "Caprese skewers to start, then pulled pork tacos with guacamole, and rice."

Lisandra rubbed her stomach. "I can't wait. I'm hungry."

"Me, too," Nissa told her, moving toward the bar. "Lavender cosmopolitans. Very fancy."

"Only the best for my ladies."

As he poured ingredients into the shaker, he felt her lightly brush his arm. Just a quick touch, to connect them. Once again he looked into her eyes and saw nothing there but happy affection. So what the hell had been going on earlier?

Once everyone had their drinks, they all took their seats. Hilde brought out a couple of bowls of tortilla chips with regular salsa and pineapple salsa.

Roberta took a chip and scooped up pineapple salsa, then took a bite.

"That's delicious," she said before turning to Coreen. "So, dear, how long have you and Shane been going out? And where did you meet?" She glanced at her son. "Some people keep their personal life far too quiet for my taste."

Coreen blushed and ducked her head. "We, ah, met at the hospital where I work."

Shane put his arm around her. "I'd seen her a few times but she was always so busy. I couldn't figure out how to approach her. Then I saw her at the Starbucks, so I waited until they called her name and I reached for her coffee at the same time."

Roberta pressed a hand to her chest. "That's so romantic. Was it love at first sight?"

Coreen blushed harder. Desmond saw Nissa straighten, her expression sympathetic.

"So I had an interesting day," she said, holding up her drink. "Maybe interesting is the wrong word."

"What happened?" Shane asked quickly in what Desmond would guess was an attempt to distract his mother from grilling Coreen.

"It turns out I'm a terrible sign dancer."

"A what?" her father asked.

Nissa laughed. "Sign dancer. You know, those people who wear a costume, hold a sign and dance on street corners."

Roberta looked concerned. "Nissa, we love you so much but you don't have much rhythm. Why would you be a sign dancer?"

"Just a temporary job, Mom. But you're right. I was terrible at it, plus it's really hard to hold a sign like that for hours and hours. I kept getting all kinds of comments." She grinned. "Some of them weren't very helpful. Even though I did my best, it wasn't a good fit for me, so I quit. I'll find something else. It's just for a few weeks, until school starts."

Desmond listened intently, waiting to see if she would say what else had happened while she was sign dancing.

"I would have loved to have seen that," Shane said.

"Oh, you would have just mocked me and driven on." She picked up her drink, then put it down. "But I did get to talk to someone really unexpected. James saw me and stopped to talk for a few minutes."

Her parents looked at her. Shane's brows drew together and Marisol tensed.

"James?" Marisol asked. "What did he want?"

Her protective tone told Desmond that Nissa hadn't said anything about James to her best friend. That had to be good news.

Nissa waved. "It was fine. Don't worry. I'm glad we got to speak. He wanted to let me know that he's found someone special and they're engaged. Her name is Cami and he seems really happy."

Her mother didn't look convinced. "Anything else?"

"Nothing." Nissa smiled. "I was happy for him and relieved. I always felt guilty about not wanting to set a date for the wedding when we were engaged."

"It was a sign," Roberta said firmly. "You weren't thrilled to be getting married. I was so sad when you broke up but it's obviously been for the best."

"That's what I said," Nissa told her. "I'm glad James and I got the chance to talk about what happened. I was happy to see him and to hear about Cami. They're getting married in about six weeks and going to Tahiti for their honeymoon."

"Tahiti?" Barry shuddered. "That's a long flight."

Roberta patted his leg. "For you, dear. Some people don't mind flying."

"I don't want to go anywhere I can't get to by car or boat," Barry grumbled. "Planes fall out of the sky."

"Ignore him," Roberta told Coreen. "Barry's a retired ferry captain. Given the choice, he would always go by boat. The only way I got him to Europe was to drive to New York and take a cruise ship across." She sighed happily. "But it was the trip of a lifetime. Every day was magical."

Conversation shifted to other forms of transportation and who had been to Europe, but Desmond kept his attention on Nissa. She was listening and laughing, completely relaxed and happy. As if nothing had happened. Which it apparently had not.

He'd been an idiot, worrying about Nissa seeing James. While they had never defined their relationship, she wasn't the type to be with two men at once. He knew that because he knew her. So why

had he worried? Why had he immediately thought
the worst? And perhaps most important of all, if he
was so sure he didn't have a heart, then why had he
cared in the first place?

NISSA

Nissa enjoyed visiting with her parents and having Shane and Coreen hang out. Everyone stayed up
too late, not wanting the fun evening to end. It was
after midnight when they called it a night.

While Coreen was saying good-night to Barry and
Roberta, Nissa pulled her brother aside.

"You seem happy," she told him, careful to keep
her voice low. "Things still going well?"

"They are." He glanced over his head toward his
date. "She's pretty amazing."

"She is. So no more games?"

He looked at her. "No more games," he agreed.
"I kind of freaked out that night. I feel dumb about
what happened."

"What did happen? Who hurt you so badly that
you weren't willing to trust Coreen?"

"The who doesn't matter, but obviously someone
betrayed me. It was a long time ago, Nissa. I was in
medical school."

"Why didn't I know?"

He touched her cheek. "Because I was played for

a fool and I didn't want to talk about it. I promised myself I would never trust again. But that's a lonely way to live."

"You men and your absolutes. What is it with that?"

He grinned. "We're quirky."

Coreen joined them along with Nissa and Shane's parents, cutting off any further chance for conversation.

Once Shane and Coreen had left, Nissa made sure her parents were settled. When she checked on the twins, they were already in bed and asleep. She hesitated outside of Desmond's room, but then didn't knock or go inside, instead retreating to her own. Sneaking around didn't seem like a safe bet with the house so full. Getting caught with Desmond would raise a lot of questions that she wasn't prepared to answer which, sadly, meant sleeping alone.

On the bright side, whatever had been bothering him when he'd first gotten home had worked itself out. By dinner, he was his normal friendly, charming self. Plus, now she understood her brother a little better. She was grateful he was letting himself fall for Coreen.

She took off her makeup and brushed her teeth, then crawled into bed, grateful that she could sleep in if she wanted.

She drifted off instantly only to be awakened two hours later by the night nurse shaking her.

Nissa sat up and stared at her. "What's wrong?" she asked, knowing there was no good reason for Marisol's nurse to be in her room at—she glanced at the clock on her nightstand—two thirty in the morning.

"I'm sorry to bother you, but Marisol is running a fever. It came on quickly and it's still climbing. I'm worried her body is rejecting the transplant. I've called her doctor and he wants her to come to the hospital right away."

Nissa was already moving. She got out of bed and flipped on the overhead light.

"Is she responsive?" she asked, ignoring the fear that exploded inside of her. She had to stay focused. She could give in to terror later.

"She's getting less so. I'm about to call an ambulance."

"Don't. At this time of night, we can get her there faster by driving her ourselves. Go wake Desmond, please. Tell him we need to take her to the hospital. I'll be downstairs in two minutes."

Nissa bolted for the bathroom. She splashed water on her face, then quickly pulled on clothes. She grabbed her purse before hurrying to her parents' room. Her mother woke up as soon as she entered.

"What's wrong?" Roberta asked.

Nissa quickly explained about Marisol. Her

mother got up at once, pulling a robe on over her nightgown.

"Are you going to tell the girls?"

Nissa shook her head. "Let's get her to the hospital first and find out what's happening. If it's bad…" Nissa swallowed against rising dread. "If it's serious and she's in danger, I'll call and you can bring the girls. It might be nothing." She prayed it was nothing, but didn't know if that was possible.

"I'll stay in touch," she promised. "Try to go back to sleep."

"I'll sleep later," her mother said firmly. "I'll go watch TV in your room. That's where the girls will go if one of them wakes up. I don't want them to find your room empty."

Her father had slept through the entire conversation. As they moved into the hall, her mother hugged her.

"I'll be praying," Roberta promised.

Nissa hugged her before running down the stairs. Desmond was already there, carrying a nearly unconscious Marisol out to the car. Nissa followed. The nurse was on the phone, letting the hospital know they were on their way.

Desmond drove quickly, obeying the stoplights, but speeding where he could. The lack of traffic meant the trip was made in half the usual time. Nissa watched her phone, waiting for instructions from the nurse. When the screen lit up, she read the message.

"We're to drive up to the emergency entrance," she said. "Don't park. A team will be waiting."

She glanced over her shoulder. Marisol was still in the back seat. Breathing, but her eyes were closed, and she seemed unaware of what was happening.

"I'm scared," she whispered, fighting tears.

"Me, too."

She saw the hospital up ahead. Desmond followed the signs to the ER and drove directly to the entrance. As soon as he stopped the car, medical personnel swarmed the vehicle. Marisol was lifted onto a gurney and rushed into the hospital. Desmond pulled away to go park the car.

Nissa waited for him just inside the entrance. When he walked inside, she rushed to him and let him pull her close. They hung on to each other.

"We can't lose her now," she whispered against his shirt. "We just can't. She's come through the surgery. She's getting better. I don't want her to die."

"Me, either. Let's wait and see what the doctor says. Maybe it's no big deal."

She looked at him and saw the worry in his dark eyes. "You don't believe that."

"I'm trying to convince myself."

They settled in the waiting room. A few patients came and went. An ambulance pulled up with victims of a car crash. It was close to five when Marisol's doctor walked out looking exhausted but relieved. Nissa gripped Desmond's hand, telling herself not to read too much into his expression.

He sat down across from them and exhaled. "She's all right. There's no sign of rejection, which is our biggest worry. She has a virus—nothing you or I would find difficult to shake, but it's more challenging for her. She was a little dehydrated and she admitted she's been doing too much over the past few days…"

He smiled. "Something about a party going past midnight?"

Nissa winced. "That's my fault. My parents came into town and my brother and his girlfriend came over and we stayed up late."

"She can't do that right now. She needs her rest and plenty of fluids. I made that clear to her. This was a scare, but she'll be fine. She just has to be careful and take things easy for a few more weeks."

Nissa nodded, tears filling her eyes. "I'm so sorry. I didn't mean to hurt her."

Desmond put his arm around her. "It wasn't your fault."

"It's my family. I should have thought to tell her to go to bed."

Marisol's doctor shook his head. "That's on her. She needs to read her own body's signals. She was feeling good and did too much. It happens, Nissa. It's not on you. But everyone needs to keep her condition in mind."

He stood. "You can see her if you want. We're going to keep her on fluids another hour or so and then she'll be ready to go home. Where she needs to rest." His voice was kind but stern.

"We'll make sure that happens," Nissa said. "Thank you so much."

"You're welcome. We all care about Marisol. She's been through a lot. No way we're going to lose her now."

When he'd left, Marisol texted her mother to let her know what was happening. They agreed to let the girls sleep in. Hopefully by the time they were up, Marisol would be back home and asleep in her own bed. Seeing her there would make them less scared when they heard what had happened.

They made their way back to Marisol's room. An IV dripped steadily, nearly in time with the up-and-down line of her heartbeat on the monitor. As they moved close to the bed, Marisol opened her eyes and smiled at them.

"Hey, you two. Sorry if I scared you."

Nissa squeezed her hand. "You nearly gave me a heart attack. I'm glad you're feeling better."

"Me, too. I guess I got too wild last night." She grimaced. "I should have listened. My nurse came and told me I was doing too much at least three or four times, but I ignored her." She glanced around the small room. "Next time I'll do what she says. I don't want to end up here again."

"Next time she needs to force you to obey her," Nissa said firmly.

"I'm not sure dragging me across the living room is in her contract." She looked at Desmond. "You carried me to the car, didn't you?"

He nodded. "Happy to do it."

"I really do intend to start walking everywhere on my own."

Desmond moved around the bed and took her other hand. "You're fine. You have a virus and you need to rest and stay hydrated. Those are easy things to do. In a couple of days, you'll feel better. It was a cheap lesson."

"You're right. I'm lucky that's all it was." She smiled at them both. "Thank you for being my friends."

"We love you," Nissa said. "We'll always be here for you."

"I know that. It gives me strength." She cleared her throat. "All right, you two. You look terrible. I'm going to be about an hour. Why don't you get some breakfast and then come back? By then they'll be ready to release me and we can all go home and get some sleep."

"You sure you'll be all right?" Nissa asked.

Marisol waved to the door. "I'm fine. Go eat and have coffee. You'll feel better."

Nissa looked at Desmond, who nodded.

"Text me if you need anything," Nissa said. "We won't be long."

Marisol said she would and they left. In the hall-way, Desmond put his arm around her.

"You doing okay?" he asked.

"Yes. She looks good and hearing from the doctor was very reassuring."

"You know what would make you feel even better? There's a fast-food place down the street. We could go get a breakfast sandwich."

She smiled at him. "You know I love a breakfast sandwich."

He chuckled. "Yes, I do."

Chapter Twelve

DESMOND

Desmond was relieved when life quickly returned to normal. Marisol got plenty of rest and fluids and within a couple of days was feeling much better. The twins had been spared the worst of the ordeal. As everyone had hoped, they slept until after their mom was back home. They'd been told what had happened, but seeing their mom right there, looking better than she had, helped them deal with the information.

Late Saturday morning, he stepped onto the deck to join Marisol. Nissa and her parents had taken the girls to the Woodland Park Zoo for the day.

He set down two glasses of lemonade and sat in the lounge chair next to her. The temperature was perfect—midseventies, with only a few clouds in the sky. They were out of the sun and Marisol had a blanket across her legs.

"You're spoiling me," she said, picking up the glass and smiling at him. "Don't stop. I really like it. I'm just pointing out the fact that I've noticed."

"You're feeling better."

"I am. I'm seeing my doctor on Monday, but I'm sure he's going to tell me the virus is gone. I'm sleeping through the night and my energy is coming back." Her humor faded. "Sorry I scared everyone. I'm being more careful."

"Screwing up is how we learn."

"I know I learned my lesson. I'm going to do everything my doctor tells me. I don't want another trip to the ER. I'm also ready to go home. Not that you haven't been a welcoming host."

"You can stay as long as you'd like, but I do understand wanting to be in your own place. Just a few more days."

Not only because she needed to recover, but there was still work to do at the house. The kitchen was finished, as was the upstairs addition, but they were waiting on a few fixtures and a couple of pieces of furniture. The plan was for Marisol and the girls to go home next Friday.

"I'm ready to be there now, but it makes sense to wait. I need to be a little stronger to manage on my own."

"You'll have a night nurse for the first couple of weeks."

She looked at him. "Desmond, no. That's ridiculous. You've already paid for too much. I don't need a nurse."

He picked up his lemonade and smiled at her. "Too bad. One's going to be there regardless."

"You're a difficult man."

"So I've been told."

"And a generous one. You've been very good to me and I don't know why."

"I'm in a position where I can help. It makes me happy to do so. Besides, we're friends."

"We are." She smiled. "Thank you. Being here rather than in a skilled nursing facility has been a blessing. And you've been so kind to the girls."

"Not being kind," he told her. "I like them. They're fun to be with. We're all going out on the water tomorrow, and Captain Pete is going to start teaching them how to drive the boat."

"That's a terrifying thought," she said with a laugh. "They are relaxed and happy. That makes my heart glad. They've been so worried about me when they should just be worried about being kids."

She frowned. "Oh, I've been meaning to ask. What's the deal with my house?"

The unexpected question surprised him. He wasn't sure what she meant or how to answer.

"I don't know what you're talking about," he said, hoping he didn't sound evasive.

"I heard the girls mention something about a new sofa and how they hoped it was comfortable. You did something, didn't you?"

He swore silently, not sure how much she knew or how to misdirect her. Perhaps some version of the truth was the easiest solution.

"I bought you a new sofa. It's a sectional with a built-in chaise. I thought you'd need something like that to help you recover. That way you don't have to go lie down every time you want to rest for a few minutes. You can sit with the twins on the sofa and be a part of things."

Tears filled her eyes. "That's so thoughtful. You're a good, good man."

"It's a sofa, Marisol. Nothing to get too excited about."

He thought she might push back on that, but she surprised him by saying, "You don't like me saying you're kind or nice, do you?"

"I, ah, it makes me uncomfortable."

"Because you're supposed to be a badass?"

He chuckled. "I have never thought of myself as a badass."

"You know what I mean. Macho and tough."

"I lean more toward contained and self-sufficient."

She sipped her drink. "Given that, how are you dealing with the house invasion? It's hard to be contained with two ten-year-old girls running around, not to mention nursing staff and Nissa's parents."

"I like having people around."

"Then why don't you make that happen on a permanent basis?"

He smiled. "Invite random strangers to move in? That would be awkward for all of us."

"Not strangers. Regular people. Why aren't you married?"

The blunt question surprised him. "I was. It didn't work out."

"Yes, I know about Rosemary the Awful." She smiled. "That's what Nissa and I call her. It's the marrying for money thing. I don't get it. There's an old saying that if you marry for money, you're going to earn every dollar. Marriage is supposed to be about loving someone."

"The way you loved your husband?" he asked, then shrugged. "Nissa mentioned you lost him a few years ago."

"Yes, like I loved him. He was a good man and we were devastated by the loss. If I hadn't had my girls, I'm not sure I would have been able to go on. But they needed me so I had to at least pretend to keep it all together. After a while, I wasn't pretending anymore, but I still miss him every day."

He believed that. Life had been hard for her—first losing her husband, then fearing for her life as she waited for a transplant. He didn't want to think about what might have happened if one hadn't come through.

"I don't miss Rosemary," he said.

"I should hope not. But that doesn't answer the question. Why haven't you fallen in love with someone else and gotten married again?"

Not a question he wanted to answer.

"I'm not the marrying kind."

She pointed at her face. "Do I look like I believe that?"

"That doesn't mean it's not true."

"What about having children? Don't you need heirs?"

He did—for the company. His parents had certainly been on him about that during their brief visit. And he wanted children in his life. Having the twins around had only confirmed that.

"I don't have a heart."

He hadn't meant to say that, but somehow the words had slipped out. He expected Marisol to roll her eyes or tease him, but she didn't. Instead she nodded slowly.

"So that's the problem?" she asked. "You don't think you're capable of love?"

"Yes. I keep people at a distance. I've done it all my life. It's what I know. Rosemary married me for the lifestyle and the money, but I've realized I married her because she checked all the boxes. I never loved her. I don't get close to anyone."

Marisol laughed. "Uh-huh. Sure. We'll ignore how you feel about Shane and his parents, but I can't not mention Nissa. You care about her. Plus, there's all that fun stuff you're doing behind closed doors. I'm guessing there's not a lot of distance there."

"How did you know?"

"I might be recovering from surgery, but I still have eyes. I've seen the way you two look at each other. There's some naked business going on for sure. So not that kind of distance?"

"I'm talking emotionally."

"You're telling me you don't let people get close and you don't want to be close to them. But you're right there with my girls and you're letting me stay here for as long as I need. Not to mention Nissa and her parents. You've opened your home to all of us, and you're taking care of everyone. Those are not the actions of a man who doesn't have a heart. Are you in love with her?"

There was no need to ask who the "her" was. "No."

"Just like that? You don't want to think about your answer first?"

"I don't love her. I can't. She needs a good man in her life, someone who can love her with his entire heart. I can't do that and I won't hurt her."

He thought Marisol might push back, but instead she simply smiled at him. "That's a whole lot of worry for a man who claims he can't care."

"I'm not a monster."

"No, you're not, but you are hiding from the truth, Desmond. You care more than you think and I can't help but wonder if that's the real problem."

She was wrong, he knew that, but saying that wouldn't convince her. The easier path was to let her believe what she would and let the rest take care of itself.

NISSA

Nissa pressed her hand to her stomach. Nerves had been growing for the past couple of days and now they were just plain acting out. For the past two days, she'd been questioning the decision to surprise Marisol with a remodeled house. They hadn't ever talked to her about it—what if she didn't want a bunch of strangers messing with her stuff? What if she hated everything they'd done? What if she blamed Nissa for all of it and stopped being her friend? And perhaps most important of all, why hadn't she thought about all this *before* the work had begun rather than after?

"It seemed like a good idea at the time," she whispered to herself as she finished getting dressed. The twins were excited and had been bursting to tell their mom what had happened. Her parents had been to the house a couple of times already and were thrilled with the changes. But none of that mattered if Marisol wasn't pleased.

Nissa went downstairs. Her parents and Desmond were sitting at the table, finishing breakfast. She took one look at the food on their plates and felt her stomach lurch. No way she was eating anything, she thought, pouring herself a cup of coffee.

"Are you all right?" her mother asked, eyeing her. "You're really pale."

"I'm fine. Just a little apprehensive about what's going to happen today."

"Second thoughts?" her father asked. "You should have considered them before you ripped off her garage roof and built a second story."

"Barry!" Roberta glared at him. "That doesn't help."

"I'm teasing." Her dad flashed her a grin. "The house is great."

Nissa glanced toward the doorway. "Where's Marisol?"

"She's already eaten," Desmond told her. "She's getting in an early therapy appointment before we load up the cars and take her home. She can't hear us."

"Good." Nissa sat at the table, doing her best to avoid looking at any of the food. "We've kept the secret this long. I don't want to ruin that now." Besides, if Marisol was going to yell at her, Nissa would prefer to put that off, as well.

"She's going to love it," Desmond told her. "The twins were very clear about what she likes and doesn't like. We didn't push back on that."

"I'm less concerned about elements of the design than the entire project." She drew in a breath. "There's no going back now. It's done." She tried to smile. "Thank you for taking the day off work."

When the time came, they would load up his car and her parents' Explorer to transport everyone to the house.

"I wouldn't miss the big reveal," he said, his voice teasing.

"I hope it goes okay," she murmured, also hoping that at the end of the day, she and Marisol were still friends.

Two hours later, everyone pitched in to carry suitcases, clothes and toys to the two vehicles.

"We've accumulated way too much stuff," Marisol said, watching the loading process from a bench in the foyer.

She'd been instructed not to carry anything heavier than a throw pillow, and Roberta was keeping an eye on her to make sure she complied. Between Nissa, Desmond, Barry and the twins, it didn't take too many trips to load the two vehicles.

"I'll bring over anything you've forgotten," Nissa told her friend.

Marisol studied her. "You feeling all right?"

Nissa faked a smile. "Never better."

"You don't look right."

"It's my stomach," Nissa admitted, thinking it was the truth. The writhing was still there, and getting more violent by the second. "Maybe something I ate."

"You sure you're up to this move?" her friend asked. "You can stay behind if you'd like. It's not as if you haven't seen my house before."

Nissa managed a slight laugh. "I want to get you settled at home." Once that happened, however the situation played out, she would feel better…or possibly worse. Either way, there would be a change.

Marisol slowly walked to Desmond's car. The twins got in the back and Nissa rode with her parents. As they'd discussed in advance, Barry left first with Desmond fake forgetting something in the house so his car arrived about five minutes later. That way Barry, Roberta and Nissa could be waiting in the driveway and not miss Marisol's reaction.

Nissa did her best not to throw herself across the back seat and beg to be put out on the side of the road. They'd done what they'd done and if Marisol was upset, she was going to have to deal with it like a grown-up.

Quicker than she would have liked, they arrived. As they got out of the SUV, she looked at the house and thought whatever happened, the place looked fantastic.

The railings had been replaced, and the front door was now a deep blue. The new windows gleamed in the perfect summer morning. The old shrubs had been replaced with bright green hedges and the grass had been fertilized and reseeded. The second story over the garage blended seamlessly with the house's roofline.

Her mother hugged her. "You did a good thing for your friend."

"It was mostly Desmond. He paid for it all and his team did the work."

"However it happened, she's going to be delighted."

Desmond's car pulled into the driveway. Nissa kept her gaze on Marisol, waiting for the moment her friend noticed all the changes. But Marisol was busy unfastening her seat belt. She climbed out of the car.

"I can't believe I'm finally home," she said with a laugh, turning around to help the girls out of the back seat. "Not that you weren't a gracious host, Desmond, but home is where—"

She stopped talking and stared at her house, first at the porch, then at the lawn and hedges.

"What did you do?"

The twins each grabbed a hand.

"Mom, you have to come see! Everything's different and it's so beautiful." Rylan practically danced in place.

Lisandra pulled her toward the porch. "It's like on TV!"

Marisol looked from the house to Nissa and Desmond. "What did you two do?"

"It wasn't just them," Lisandra told her. "It was us and Erica and everybody."

"Who's Erica?"

"Perhaps not the point," Desmond said drily, and walked to the front door. "Shall we?"

He opened the front door, then stepped back. The girls led Marisol inside the house. Nissa followed, hoping it was going to go well.

Light spilled in through the new windows, and the hardwood floors gleamed. There was a big overstuffed sectional in a pretty blue-green fabric and lots of pillows and a few throws. A couple of club chairs provided additional seating, and on the wall above the refurbished fireplace was a new big-screen TV.

To the right was the dining room. Marisol's big table was still there, but a new hutch filled the long wall, providing tons of storage. New linens and dishes were in place on the table and on the living room side of the huge two-level island.

Marisol pressed a hand to her mouth as tears filled her eyes. "You redid my house."

Nissa bit her bottom lip, not sure if that was an informational statement, a complaint or happiness.

"It's so beautiful," Marisol added, turning to Nissa. "Everyone did this for me?"

"Who else?" Nissa asked, moving close and hugging her. "You're not mad?"

"Mad? You've made this my dream house. I can't believe you did this."

She held out her arm to Desmond, who joined them in a three-way hug. The twins danced impatiently around them.

"There's more," Rylan said eagerly. "You have to see it all."

They went into the kitchen where Marisol ran her hands along the stunning quartz countertops. The girls pointed out the new appliances and the pull-out drawers in the lower cabinets. Marisol admired the new pots and pans and agreed she liked the dishes very much.

They went out back. New outdoor furniture sat on the new covered deck. A stainless steel barbecue stood in one corner and all the plants had been replaced with hardy, regional favorites.

Returning to the house, the twins took her down the short hall that had led to the two bedrooms. Marisol came to a stop as she pointed.

"There are stairs." She spun to face Desmond. "You gave me a second story?"

He grinned. "You didn't notice it when we drove in?"

"No. I was too busy looking at the yard and my front door." She pressed a hand to her chest, as if trying to catch her breath. "No wonder my physical therapist has been pushing me to work on my thigh strength. She knew about the stairs."

Nissa opened the door to the half bath tucked under the stairs, then pointed to the door leading to the master.

"You might want to check that out."

Marisol began to cry again when she saw her refurbished bedroom. The furniture was all new, as was the area rug over the hardwood floors. The girls showed her the remodeled bathroom and the new walk-in closet.

Nissa's throat tightened a little as she watched her friend's happy reaction.

"I was terrified she would be mad," she admitted to her mother.

"You did everything with love. She knows that."

They all returned to the base of the stairs. Desmond picked up Marisol and carried her to the second story. Once on the landing, he put her down.

"I'm going to get busy building up my strength," she said firmly. "I want to be able to get up here myself."

"You will," he told her, nodding at the two doors. "Take a look."

The girls' rooms were mirror images of each other. There was a big window, one overlooking the front of the house and the other overlooking the back. A comfy chair was tucked in the corner by the window and a desk was next to it. Bookshelves stood on either side of the closet door.

Against the north wall stood the loft-style bunk bed, with a full bed on the bottom, a built-in chest of drawers at one end and a twin bed up top. Rylan had done her room in shades of blue, while Lisandra had chosen purple as her main color.

Barry looked around. "Good use of space," he said. "Quality materials."

"It's lovely," Roberta added.

Marisol nodded, wiping away tears. "I can't take

it all in." She looked at Desmond. "I don't know how to thank you."

"Be happy and healthy. That's all I need."

"This is so wonderful," Marisol murmured. "It's like a dream."

"Except it's real!" Rylan shouted.

Everyone laughed, then started downstairs. Marisol insisted on going on her own. She went slowly, but made it to the main floor.

"Let's unload the car," Nissa said.

Marisol pointed to the stairs. "I'm going to start practicing while you do that. Five stairs today, six tomorrow, until I can make it upstairs on my own." She laughed. "My physical therapist will be so proud of me."

Nissa wanted to say she didn't have to push herself, but knew that Marisol would want to be able to reach her kids in case something happened.

They brought in all the suitcases and tote bags. It didn't take long to get it all put away. By then Marisol had finished her five stairs and was exploring the kitchen. Nissa showed her where the manuals had been stashed.

"You'll need to learn how to use your fancy new appliances," Nissa teased.

"I will. And I'm having you both over for dinner, just as soon as I'm comfortable standing long enough to cook."

Desmond leaned against the island. "Don't worry about that. I set you up with a meal delivery service through the end of September." He glanced at his watch. "You should already have an email from them telling you about the program. Nissa and Roberta picked out the first two nights' choices, but after that, you can choose from a wide selection."

"So much for not having a heart," Marisol said before hugging him.

Marisol looked at Nissa. "Thank you. It's the most wonderful surprise ever."

Nissa looked around at the beautiful new house and knew her friend was right. Not because of the things that had been purchased, but because of the love that would always live here.

Chapter Thirteen

NISSA

A few days after the fantastic house reveal, Nissa found herself feeling oddly restless. She had no idea of the cause, but she couldn't shake the sense of something being not right. She liked her temp job—she was working in a small bakery where the owner's daughter had to unexpectedly go on bed rest for the last two months of her pregnancy. Nissa was learning all about decorating cakes and cookies, not to mention working the front counter. The money was good, the owners warm and friendly. So her problem wasn't the job.

And it wasn't missing Marisol. She'd already been over to the house several times. The twins were settling in to their new rooms and her friend could make it up the stairs on her own. Everyone was happy and healthy, so they weren't what was making her feel almost itchy inside her skin.

She wandered through Desmond's large house, as if she'd left the answer in one of the beautiful rooms, but there was nothing to be found. Finally, she went into her parents' room. Her father was out golfing with Shane while her mother packed them up for their trip back home.

Nissa knocked once on the open door before walking in and sitting in the chair in the corner. Her mother looked up from the pair of jeans she was folding.

"You're troubled," Roberta said, putting down the jeans and settling on the bed. "What's wrong?"

"I don't know. I can't seem to settle."

Her mother nodded. "I know the feeling. Restlessness with a vague sense of dread."

"That describes it, but I don't know the cause, so I can't fix it. Maybe I should start a regular exercise program."

Her mother laughed. "While that would be healthy, I doubt it will solve the problem."

"I know, but it might be a distraction. I just can't figure out what's wrong. I'm ready for the new school year and I'm excited about my students. The temp job is fun and interesting. I'm saving plenty of money for my trip next summer. My renters have sent a couple of emails saying what a good time they're having. Marisol's doing great, you and Dad are healthy. So what's my problem?"

"You really don't know?"

Nissa shook her head. "Do you?"

"You're in love with Desmond."

Nissa half rose out of the chair, only to collapse back on the seat. Her mind went completely blank as she momentarily forgot how to breathe. It was as if her entire being had to reboot.

"What? No. In love with him? I can't be."

Her mother watched her with that "I'm going to be patient because I love my child, but wow is she dumb" look.

"Why would you think that?" Nissa asked. "It's ridiculous. We're friends."

Friends who slept together, Nissa thought, wondering if her mother had figured out what was going on the way Marisol had. She wasn't about to ask. Discussing love was one thing, but sex wasn't a topic she wanted to share with her mother.

"Nissa, you've had feelings for Desmond since you were fourteen years old. At first I was sure it was just a crush, but they never fully went away. Now you've been living with him and spending time with him. It makes sense that what you'd had before would grow into something bigger."

"It doesn't make sense to me," she admitted, emotionally poking at her heart to try to find out what was happening in there. In love with Desmond. Could she be? Did she want to be?

"I like him a lot," she said slowly. "He's kind and funny and generous and we have fun together. He's a really great guy. I trust him. But that's not love."

She looked at her mother. "His parents hate me."

"No, they don't."

"His mother does. Evelyn told me that I wouldn't in any way be an asset to him and that he would break my heart." She frowned, trying to remember the exact words. "Okay, maybe not that, but it wasn't good."

"Desmond isn't close to his family. He's not going to care what they think."

"He might care a little. Mom, I can't be in love with him. It would ruin everything."

"How so?"

"He doesn't think he has a heart."

She expected her mother to scoff at the suggestion, but Roberta surprised her by nodding slowly.

"I can see how he would think that. Of course not having a heart isn't the problem. It's that his heart has been broken over and over again."

Nissa raised her eyebrows. "Since when? He's

never been dumped. He's the one who ended things with Rosemary."

"Yes, but why? It's not as if he suddenly decided he didn't want to be married to her. Desmond figured out why she'd married him. He saw she was only in it for the money and not for the man. How do you think that made him feel?"

She'd never thought about the situation from that perspective. "He would have been upset." Hurt, certainly. She wasn't sure that he'd ever truly loved Rosemary, but regardless, the end of the marriage would have been difficult.

"Let's go back a little in time," her mother said. "What about all those young women who tried to get his attention because he was rich and not because of who he was?"

"You know about that?"

"It doesn't take a genius to know it happened over and over again. Before them, he was dealing with his parents. They weren't exactly nurturing when it came to their son. He was raised by a series of nannies until he was sent off to boarding school. Who loved him then? It might be easier for Desmond to tell you he doesn't have a heart, but the truth is, his has been shattered and he's afraid to trust."

Nissa tried to take it all in. Her mother's words made sense, she thought. It wasn't about him loving so much as him trusting himself enough to risk caring about someone. About her.

That last thought surprised her. Was that the problem? She didn't know how he felt about her? Oh, she knew he liked her and they were good friends, but none of that would upset her. The real problem was much bigger because there was so much potential for everything to go wrong. Staying friends with Desmond would be easy but falling in love with him would change everything.

"Loving him isn't a good idea," Nissa said, still easing into acceptance.

"Oh, I don't know. You've waited for him for a long time. Don't you think you're due for a little happiness?"

"You're ignoring everything we just talked about. Desmond can't or won't love me back."

"That's what he said," her mother told her. "Let's wait and see what he does. A man's actions often have a lot more significance. He didn't help Marisol just because he's a nice guy, he helped her because he wanted to do something nice for your friend. You're at the center of everything that's happened."

Nissa wished that were true, but she was having a hard time believing Desmond saw her as more than a friend he liked in his bed. As for her feelings…

She thought about how she felt when she was around him and how he'd always been the best man she'd ever known. She thought about his kindness and thoughtfulness, how he made her laugh and how she knew, when something bad happened, that he would be there. She thought about how she wanted to take care of him and be there for him, so he would know, no matter what, that she had his back.

"Oh, no," she whispered. "I'm in love with him."

Her mother smiled. "I'm just so proud. Now what are you going to do?"

"You mean after I throw up?"

"Yes, after that."

"I'm going to tell him." She had no idea where she would get the courage, but she was going to do it. She had to. After everything that had happened to him, Desmond needed to know she loved him fully and truly, with no reservations. Not for the money or anything else, but just for himself.

NISSA

Nissa's parents left an hour later. She spent the rest of the morning trying to get her courage together, only to fail a thousand times. It was close to three when she finally got herself downstairs and heading for his office. She was going to do it, she told herself. She was going to confess her feelings. With a little luck he would sweep her into his arms and tell her

he felt exactly the same, then whip out an engagement ring and get down on one knee.

Okay, that last bit was unlikely—most men didn't
keep a diamond ring in a spare drawer, just in case
they needed to get engaged. But having him tell her
he loved her back would be great. Or if not that, then
at least maybe he could mention he liked her a lot
and wanted to go out with her and be in a serious
relationship that would lead to love. Any other option was going to be difficult to handle, but she was
determined to be mature. Or at least not beg.

She saw his office door stood open. That had to
be a good sign, she told herself, not that she could
remember a time when it had been closed, but still.
She would take all the good signs she could get. She
wiped her suddenly sweaty hands on her shorts, then
cleared her throat and walked directly into his office.

"Hey, Desmond," she began, only to come to a
stop when she saw his expression.

He didn't look happy to see her as he stared at
her from across his desk. In fact he looked kind of
scrunchy, as if he was upset about something. No,
not upset. That was the wrong word. So was mad, but
she immediately knew there was a problem.

"What happened?" she asked. "Is everything all
right?"

Emotion flashed in his eyes, but was gone before
she could figure out what he was thinking.

"I don't want you to be in love with me."

"Wh-what?"

She managed to speak that single word before all her air rushed out and the room began to spin. The only way she stayed upright was by grabbing the back of the visitor's chair and telling herself to breathe.

"I don't want you to be in love with me," he repeated, his voice firm and completely lacking in any feeling. He might as well have been telling her that quarterly taxes were due in two weeks.

"But how did you—"

"I overheard you talking to your mother earlier."

Heat rushed to her face as humiliation swept through her. "You were there?"

"In the hall. I was coming to tell your mother she had several things in the family room. I didn't want her to forget them."

He sounded so formal, she thought as her chest tightened and her eyes burned. So distant. Gone was the man who had laughed with her, kissed her with so much passion and made every day just a little bit brighter.

"I apologize for eavesdropping."

"I hardly think that part matters." She forced herself to meet his cold gaze. "I take it you don't return my feelings."

He opened a desk drawer. For a single second,

she thought he would pull out an engagement ring. Only she knew that was wrong and when she saw what he held in his hand, she felt her heart shatter into a thousand pieces.

He stood and placed a hotel room key on the desk between them.

"I've made arrangements for you to stay there for the rest of the summer. It's a suite, so you'll have plenty of room. You can check in now. Hilde will bring you your things."

He was getting rid of her, she thought, ready to go numb anytime now. Because hurting as much as she did was going to be unendurable in the long term.

"You want me gone that quickly," she said, knowing he could hear the pain in her voice.

"You're welcome to pack them yourself," he said stiffly. "I thought you'd prefer to go as soon as possible."

She looked from him to the key and back. "I'm not running from you, Desmond. I'm sorry you feel the way you do about what's happening. Regardless, I think the hotel room is a little dramatic. You could have just said you weren't interested in me that way. I would have gotten the message."

She took a step back. "I won't need the hotel room, although the offer is generous. I'll get my things together and be out of here within the hour." She looked at him, memorizing his handsome face and wondering how long it would be before she saw him smile again.

"I appreciate what a gracious host you've been. Until today, the summer has been amazing and you've been a big part of that. What we had together..." She tried to collect her thoughts. The pain was still there, but it was contained by a new confidence and a certainty that she'd done nothing wrong.

"I've been in love with you a long time," she said softly. "Probably from the night of my prom. The feelings got buried, but they were still there. James wasn't wrong when he accused me of being too involved in your life, but I couldn't see what he was talking about."

She walked to the door, then turned back. "I'm not sure what you're afraid of. I get that you'd have trouble believing someone loved you, what with your parents and learning Rosemary was only in it for the money. But what about you and Shane? You've been friends for years. You love each other." She managed a slight smile. "In a very manly way, of course."

He didn't react to her words and her smile faded.

"My parents have been devoted to you," she continued. "And even ignoring my recent declaration, I've been very consistent about being your friend. I'm sad after all this time, you still won't trust us."

She paused, only to realize that there was nothing left to say. She'd been honest and had told him everything, and none of it had changed his mind.

"Goodbye, Desmond."

DESMOND

Desmond saw the determination in Nissa's eyes and the strength in her body. She'd laid herself bare to him and she wasn't afraid. No matter what happened, she was going to be honest to the end and accept the consequences. He wasn't sure he'd known anyone that brave.

"I don't want to hurt you," he said.

"Too late."

"This is short term. If we stayed together, I would destroy you. Everything seems fine now, but eventually you'd figure out that I'm just like my parents. That I don't have a heart and that even if I wanted to love you back, I don't know how. That would eat away at you, over time. I don't want that for you."

She smiled at him. "Really? This is for my own good? It's not like you to lie, Desmond."

"I'm telling the truth. You don't know who I am. Not deep down inside."

"I know you better than you think. I'm going to tell you something that is going to make you angry and you're not going to have anywhere to put that anger, which will frustrate you. You'll want to protect me, even more than you do now, and that will only make this situation more difficult for both of us."

"I doubt it can be much more difficult," he told her.

"Want to bet?" She raised a shoulder. "Remember the Chihuly event? How your parents came?"

"Yes." Although he had no idea how they related to any of this.

"Your mother and I had a little chat. She told me that I shouldn't get my hopes up. That you wouldn't be interested in me because I didn't bring anything to the table, so to speak. I couldn't help you in business or socially and I didn't belong in your world."

Anger erupted. "She had no right to say that."

"But say it, she did."

The anger grew and bubbled, making him want— He swore quietly. He wanted to protect her, just like she'd said. He was furious and frustrated and he wanted to take on the world, only that wouldn't do any good.

"You guessing what would happen doesn't change anything," he told her.

"I didn't guess." She drew in a breath. "You're wrong about all of it, Desmond. You're missing the entire point. If you were like your parents, if you were as heartless as you claim, why would my loving you make a difference in what was happening between us? Me loving you should only enhance the lovemaking, so in theory, you should be taking advantage of me. So what if I get my heart broken? It doesn't matter to you. Heartless people aren't moved by that sort of thing. But you do care about me, perhaps more than you want to. I'm not the problem. You are."

She shook her head. "I didn't see that before now, but it's true. You find it easy to write a check because that's safe. But giving of yourself, that's the hard thing. Because when you give, you take a risk that you'll be rejected. The only way to know love is to give love, and that's what you've been unable to do. It's not about the money or having a heart. It's about being brave enough to risk it all."

She raised her head and squared her shoulders. "I love you, Desmond, but you're right. I don't belong here. Not anymore. I need to be with someone who's willing to fight for me. I want a man who loves me back, heart and soul. I want to be someone's everything and you can't give me that."

She pressed her lips together. He thought she might say more, but instead she turned and walked out of his office. He stood where he was, listening to her move around his house, then she walked to the stairs. He would guess she'd collected her things and now she was going to pack them and leave.

She was right to go and she was right to tell him

she didn't belong to him anymore. She was right about all of it.

Unable to watch her walk away, he left his office and got in his car. When he started driving, he had no destination in mind, but he knew he wouldn't go home for a long, long time.

NISSA

Nissa drove to Marisol's house. She'd texted to say she was on her way and her friend had said she would be waiting. She was strong and brave right up until Marisol opened the front door and said, "The girls are at a friend's house, so I'm hoping you're here to see me."

Nissa started to say that was fine, but burst into tears instead. Marisol pulled her close.

"It's that man, isn't it? I knew he was going to be trouble. Want me to call around and see if I can find someone to beat him up? I might know a few people."

Despite everything, Nissa managed a smile. "You don't know anyone to beat him up."

"Not personally, but you'd be amazed what you can find on the internet."

They went inside. Nissa was together enough to look around the house and admire how great it all looked before collapsing on the sofa.

"I'm such a fool."

"No," her friend said firmly sitting next to her. "It's not wrong to love someone. He's single, you're single and you were sleeping together. Love is kind of the next step."

"Not for him."

"Then he's the fool, not you. Tell me what happened."

Nissa explained about the conversation with her mother and her decision to suck it up and confess her feelings.

"Only he already knew," she said. "He'd overheard the whole thing and when I went into his office, he handed me a key for a hotel room. He expected me to stay there instead of with him."

"Like I said, a fool."

Nissa felt her eyes fill with tears. "I'm trying to be brave, but it hurts."

"Of course it does. He broke your heart. You know you belong together, but he's not willing to see that. At least not yet."

"You can't still have hope."

"Of course I do. I'm a romantic at heart."

Nissa supposed that was because she'd loved once. Marisol knew what it was like to give her heart and get someone else's in return. She knew about the ups and downs of any relationship and how good it felt to find the right person, even if that love didn't last as long as she'd hoped.

"Do you ever think about falling in love again?" she asked.

Marisol surprised her by shrugging. "Sometimes. At first I couldn't imagine it. But since the surgery, I'm ready to start imagining the possibility, if that makes sense. He'd have to be very special to step into our lives, but I'm hoping someone like that is out there."

Nissa squeezed her hand. "I hope so, too."

She said the words automatically, but what she was thinking was how incredibly brave her friend was. To have lost her husband, faced a terminal illness, then to have gone through transplant surgery and come out the other side still believing in love was amazing.

"I want to be like you when I grow up," she said.

Marisol laughed. "Aim higher. So what's the plan? Would you like to stay here? The girls could move into one room and you could take the other."

"Thank you but I'm going to head over the mountains. I've already texted my mom and she said they're fine with me staying there until my renters leave in a couple of weeks. I'll use the time to clear my head and get ready for the upcoming school year."

"A wise plan. What about Desmond?"

Nissa didn't want to think about him, but it was impossible. Between the ache in her heart and the fact that she already missed him, there was very little else on her mind.

"He knows how I feel," she said firmly. "What happens next is up to him."

Chapter Fourteen

DESMOND

The house echoed with silence. The Monday after Nissa had left him, Hilde had told him she needed to take a couple of weeks off to visit her family in Estonia. Desmond had bought her a business-class ticket and had assured her that he would survive in her absence. She'd arranged for someone to come in a couple of days a week to do basic cleaning and make sure there was food in the refrigerator. Not that he was eating. Or sleeping.

When he was at the office, he couldn't focus on what was happening and when he was home, he wandered from room to room, listening to the echoes of conversations he and Nissa had had on nearly every topic imaginable.

He stood by her small patch of the garden, filled with random plants and flowers that had been on sale the day they'd gone to Fred Meyer. He waited by the hidden bar in the family room, hoping to hear her footsteps on the stairs so he could fix her a cocktail. He searched for items she might have left behind—a book, a scarf, a pen—anything that he would have to return, as an excuse to go see her. Only he knew he couldn't barge into her life. She'd gotten away from him and wasn't that the point of all this? To let her go live her normal life with a normal man who would love her and cherish her and give her everything she could ever want?

Thursday afternoon, he traced a now-familiar route through the house. He'd yet to find anything she'd forgotten and the quiet no longer comforted him as it had before she'd moved into his house. Instead the rooms echoed with memories and laughter, with words he couldn't quite hear and conversations that seemed to mock him.

He hadn't eaten in days and he couldn't sleep. He would guess both of those conditions were making the situation worse. The solution to the problem seemed just out of reach. Every time he thought he was about to understand all of it, his mind went blank and he started walking the house again.

He'd just returned to the kitchen, more because he'd heard it called the heart of the home than because he was the least bit hungry, when his cell phone rang. He answered it without glancing at the screen, then wished he hadn't when he heard his mother's voice.

"I called the office, Desmond. They said you weren't in. Are you ill?"

"I'm fine, Mother, how are you?"

"I'm doing well. I have some excellent news. Do you remember Pedra Holder? She was such a beautiful girl. A brilliant pianist. She married far too young and of course the relationship failed. But she's divorced now, with two darling little boys. I had lunch with her mother and she said Pedra was asking about you."

"I have no idea who she is."

"Of course you do. You met her several times when you were home on holiday. She's tall and blonde. Oh, I'll text you a picture. You'll recognize her at once. My point is, she's back in San Francisco. I'll get you her contact information. You can fly down and take her to dinner."

"Are you setting me up?"

"Why are you asking that question? Isn't it obvious? I've been patient long enough, Desmond. You decided Rosemary wasn't the one, and all this time later, you're still single. We need heirs and Pedra is a proven breeder. We'll have to be extra careful on the prenup, of course. Make sure the two children she has won't inherit anything, but that's why we have lawyers."

He sat on the bottom stair, not sure which was more shocking. His mother referring to the daughter of a friend as a "breeder" or the assumption that he was single.

"I'm not going to be going out with Pedra or anyone else, so you don't have to worry about the lawyers."

"Why ever not? Don't tell me you're actually involved with that Nissa girl. You can't be. I'll admit she's pretty enough, but Desmond, do be sensible. She's simply not one of us. She would never fit into your lifestyle. She doesn't have the education or the socialization."

His mother lowered her voice. "If you're worried about giving up great sex, then keep her on the side. Marry Pedra to have children and use Nissa for sex. You won't be the first man to solve a problem that way."

He wondered if she thought she was being helpful. He knew she wouldn't be deliberately trying to provoke him. That wasn't her way. For his mother, life was all about position and power and making sure she achieved her desired outcome.

"Have you ever been in love?" he asked. "Truly, romantically, wildly in love?"

He expected her to immediately say no and tell him love was a nonsense word invented by sad people with sad lives as a way to get through the day. But instead she sighed.

"Yes. Once. Many years ago. One of my tutors. He was just out of college, so your grandfather didn't want to hire him, but he was a brilliant mathematician and it was only for a few weeks. His name was Marcus."

He was as surprised by the wistful tone to her voice as by what she was saying.

"You were lovers?"

"Why do men always ask about sex? Fine, yes, we were lovers, but for me it was about so much more than that. Marcus was a wonderful man with a brilliant mind. He went on to join NASA where he worked on the Space Station."

"But you didn't marry him."

"What?" Her voice sharpened. "Marry him? A penniless mathematician with no family, no prospects? And do what? Live in the suburbs in a tract home, popping out babies every three years?" She laughed. "That was not my dream at all."

"But you loved him."

"Yes, and I enjoyed our time together. Then I married your father."

"It was more of a merger than a marriage."

"Call it what you will. We've been together forty years and we've provided a very comfortable life for you. Now it's your turn to do your duty. Have children, Desmond. I've been very patient and it's past time. Call Pedra and set up something, then fly down to San Francisco and dazzle her. If things go as I hope, you can move the company back to where it belongs. Your father and I are getting tired of flying to Seattle. The weather is always miserable there."

He glanced out at the warm, sunny day. "You're right, Mother."

"About the weather, or about the rest of it?"

"About everything. It is time I married and had children. It's time for me to do a lot of things."

"Excellent. I'll text you her contact information right now. And a picture of her boys. They're charming, but as I said, they won't be inheriting. All right, Desmond. Good luck. I'll speak with you soon."

She hung up and seconds later, the contact information was delivered, along with a couple of pictures of two smiling little boys.

He ignored both as he tried to process the fact that his mother had once fallen in love. He wouldn't have thought her capable. But apparently it had happened, not that she'd let her feelings stop her from moving forward with her life. Marcus had touched her heart, but there was no way he was getting his hands on her life or her bank account.

So she *could* love, but she'd chosen not to. Duty came first. Duty and money. He supposed if he were to ask his father the same question, he would get a similar answer. For all he knew, there was a woman somewhere, his father's true love, kept in a lovely apartment. Cherished but never seen in public. It was like something out of a nineteenth-century novel.

He didn't want that, he thought. He didn't want to marry for duty and produce heirs. He didn't want to get in touch with Pedra and fly down to San Francisco to take her out. He wanted to be with Nissa. He wanted a house full of family and friends. He wanted kids running around and a messy garden with plants bought on sale. He wanted Nissa smiling at him, touching him, telling him she loved him. He wanted her so much, he wasn't sure how to survive without her.

But if he went to her and told her that, then what? What happened when she found out that he was— that he was—

"What?" he asked aloud.

What exactly was she supposed to find out? That he could be difficult and moody, that sometimes he got too involved in work? That he wasn't overly fond of his parents, but he tried to be dutiful? That she made everything better and that he'd never once in his life felt about anyone else the way he felt about her?

If he really didn't have a heart, how was it possible to miss her so much? If he didn't love her, why could he so easily see a future with her? If he wasn't a normal person with regular emotions, how could he feel sorry for his parents and the ridiculous choices they'd made?

He stood up and searched through his contacts. When he landed on the right one, he pushed the call button and waited.

"I wondered how long it would take to hear from you," Barry said, his voice a grumble. "You've made my baby girl cry. That's not something a father forgives easily."

"I know. Can you meet me for coffee?"

"You in the area?"

"I'm heading over now."

"It's a six-hour drive, son."

"Not if you charter a plane."

There was a pause before Barry said, "And that's what you're going to do?"

"I am."

"All right, then. After that, we'd best meet for a beer." He gave Desmond the name of a local bar. "See you in a couple of hours."

"I'll be there."

DESMOND

The bar wasn't much to look at from the outside, or the inside, but Desmond didn't care about that. He glanced around until he saw Barry sitting at a table in the back, a beer in front of him. Desmond paused by the bar and ordered a beer for himself, then walked toward Nissa's father. When the older man looked up and saw him, Barry's expression wasn't welcoming.

"You can't buy your way out of this," Barry told him. "Not with a fancy plane or your big boat. You hurt her. She's been crying since she got here. How do you think that makes us feel? We trusted you, Desmond. We let you into our life and our hearts. We welcomed you and this is how you've repaid us."

Each word was a kick in the gut with a few of them slashing at the heart he'd claimed not to have. As Barry glowered at him, Desmond realized that he'd been more wrong than he'd realized. Shane wasn't taking his calls, and now Barry was looking at him like he'd destroyed something important.

He supposed he had—he'd broken Nissa's heart.

"I'm sorry," he began.

Barry turned away. "I don't want to hear it."

Desmond knew that wasn't true. Barry had agreed to meet him, so he must want to hear something.

"My mother wants me to marry some socialite she knows. Pedra. She already has two boys from a previous marriage, so my mom is concerned about a prenup. The other kids shouldn't inherit any part of the family empire. She pointed out that not only was Pedra a proven breeder—and that's an actual quote—if Nissa was so important to me, I could keep her on the side."

Barry's gaze narrowed. "Don't make me take you down, son. Because I can and I will."

Desmond ignored that. "I asked her if she'd ever been in love. I already knew she didn't love my father. Theirs is a true marriage of convenience. She admitted she had, many years ago, but she wasn't the least bit tempted to stay with the man she loved. She didn't see the purpose."

He looked at Barry. "That's how I was raised. I don't say that as an excuse, but as an explanation. I grew up knowing I had a duty and that the family business was all that mattered. Growing it, being more powerful. I needed to fit in with society." He thought about all those wonderful evenings with Nissa. "How to make a great cocktail. I look good in a suit, I speak four languages, but no one ever bothered to teach me or even show me how to be a good person. No one ever talked about love or respect or treating people with decency. The little I know, I learned from you and Roberta."

"Apparently you forgot the most important lesson of all," Barry told him.

"I didn't forget it, I didn't think it applied to me. I didn't think I had a heart. It never occurred to me I could love anyone, not the way you love Roberta or she loves you. I thought I wasn't capable of those kinds of feelings and because of that, I wanted to protect Nissa from me. If she fell for me, then she would be saddled with a man who could never love her back."

One of the servers put a beer in front of him, then walked away. He moved the glass in a slow circle.

"I told myself I was sending her away for her own good. Better to end things quickly, let her get over me and have a chance at someone better."

"I'm still going to beat the crap out of you," Barry said conversationally. "Just so you know."

"Fair enough." He paused to gather his thoughts. "I was wrong about all of it. About letting her go and thinking it was better for her, about not having a heart, about being incapable of loving. I do have a heart and it's a pile of rubble right now."

He looked at Barry. "I hide behind my money. I write a check instead of getting involved. I keep my distance from people because it's what I know and therefore it's easier. The only place I've ever felt that I could truly be myself was when I was with you and your family. No. Wait. That's not true. I was myself with Nissa. When she was living with me, I was exactly who I was meant to be."

He picked up his beer, then put it down. "I love her. I think I have from the night I took her to her prom. She is an amazing woman and for reasons I don't understand, she loves me back. I don't deserve her or her heart, but she wants me to have both. I'm sorry I hurt her and that I betrayed your trust in me. I want to spend the rest of my life proving myself to both of you, and most importantly to Nissa. And I'd like your permission to ask her to marry me." He paused. "If she'll have me."

Barry took a long swallow of his beer and set down the glass. "No."

Desmond hadn't expected that. He'd thought the older man would lecture him, but the flat-out refusal hit him like a sucker punch.

"You did say you'd take me down," he murmured. "You were right."

"Let me tell you something, Desmond. You've always been like a son to me, but if you want my blessing, I'll only give it on the condition that you grovel before you ask. I mean take full responsibility. No piddly-ass 'I'm sorry if you're upset' crap. Being sorry she's upset doesn't own up to what got her that way in the first place. You need to grovel like you've never groveled before."

"Yes, sir."

Barry threw a few bills on the table. "All right, let's head home. Roberta took Nissa out to the movies. They should be getting back in the next half hour or so. You'll be waiting on the front steps." Barry grinned. "Like a homeless dog."

Desmond would have been happy to wait on the curb, he thought, following the man he hoped would be his future father-in-law outside. The where didn't matter. All that was important was seeing Nissa and telling her how sorry he was and how much he loved her.

NISSA

"Oh, that movie was so charming," Nissa's mother said with a sigh as they drove back home. "I loved it. Did you like it, dear?"

Nissa faked a smile. "Sure. It was funny."

Or at least the audience had laughed a lot. Nissa hadn't seen the humor in two people thrown together in unexpected circumstances and then falling in love. The romantic comedy had reminded her of what it had been like to be with Desmond, only for her, there hadn't been a happily-ever-after ending. Instead she was heartbroken and he was, well, she didn't know where he was but he wasn't with her.

The pain hadn't faded. She would have thought it would start to get better, but obviously more time needed to pass before that was going to happen. She thought about him constantly. At night, when she managed to fall asleep, she dreamed about him. Every part of her ached for him. She'd lost her appetite and could barely get through the day.

She was giving herself the rest of the week to wallow. On Saturday her tenants were moving out. When they were gone, she would return home and get ready for the upcoming school year. She was going to find a cheap yoga class and take an Italian course. She would hang out with her friends and cook healthy meals and just plain fake it because she knew that after a while, she wouldn't be faking it anymore. She would be healed. Right now that seemed impossible, but she'd seen how strong people could be and she was determined to act just like them.

Exhausted but fairly sure she wouldn't be able to sleep, Nissa leaned back in her seat and closed her eyes. The steady sound of the motor and the movement of the car relaxed her. She opened her eyes when she felt them turn into the driveway. Her mother stopped in front of the garage.

"Would you go around front, Nissa," she said as she got out. "I think I saw a package on the porch when we drove up."

"Sure, Mom."

Nissa slung her handbag over her shoulder and walked around to the front of the house, only to come to a stop when she saw Desmond sitting on the front porch steps. He rose when he saw her.

It was late, nearly ten, and dark. The porch light illuminated the shape of him, but not his expression. She had no idea why he was here or what she was supposed to say to him. The man had broken her heart into so many pieces, she wasn't sure it could ever be whole again and yet she wanted to run to him and hold him. She wanted to feel his body against hers, listen to his voice and tell him how much she loved him and had missed him, which made her the biggest idiot ever born.

"I'm sorry," he said, walking toward her. "I was a fool. Worse, I was cruel and unthinking and I apologize for that, as well."

He stopped in front of her. "Nissa, you are the most warm, giving person I know. You embrace the world and see only the good in people. You are funny and beautiful and there are a thousand reasons why I didn't see what was right in front of me, but I didn't. Until now. I love you. I love you and I'm so sorry for not recognizing that before. I'm sorry I hurt you and I'm sorry for what you've been through. I was totally in the wrong."

She blinked, not able to take it all in. He loved her? He *loved* her?

"What happened?" she asked, not quite able to believe.

"I talked to my mother."

"I know she's not a fan, so she can't be responsible for your change of heart."

He smiled. "She is. She wants me to marry for duty, like she did. I don't want that. I don't want a cold, sterile existence. I want plants on sale and your books everywhere. I want laughter and kids and dogs and a loud, crazy house. I want a life with you. Can you forgive me just enough to let me try to earn my way back into your world?"

Deep inside a tiny spark of hope ignited. It grew and grew until she felt the pain of missing him start to ease.

"Because you love me?" she asked.

"Yes. With all my heart. For always. I love you, Nissa, and I hope you still feel the same way about me."

"I'm not the kind of person to simply fall out of love."

"That's what I was hoping you'd say."

He leaned down and kissed her. At the feel of his mouth against hers, her heart filled with all the love it had been denied. She flung her arms around him and gave herself over to his kiss and everything it promised.

They stood on the front walkway, wrapped in each other, kissing and whispering their love for several minutes. Then Desmond stepped back and dropped to one knee.

"Nissa Lang, you are the most amazing woman

I've ever known. I love you and I promise to love you for the rest of my life. Will you marry me?"

As he spoke, he drew a small ring box out of his jeans front pocket and opened it. Inside was a sparking emerald-cut diamond set in an art deco design.

"I know this isn't traditional, but it reminded me of you," he said. "If you don't like it, I'll get you something else."

She pretended to consider the offer. "Because you couldn't get a diamond solitaire? I just don't know."

He smiled. "Nissa, did you want to answer the question?"

She tugged him to his feet, then stared into his beautiful dark eyes. "Yes, Desmond. I'll marry you. I love you. I want us to be together always."

"And the ring?"

"I love it exactly as it is."

He slid the ring on her finger. It fit perfectly, which she took as a sign.

"I can't believe this is happening," she admitted. "You really came all the way here and you love me."

"I can't believe I almost lost you."

They settled on the porch stairs, his arm around her. "Where do you want to live?"

She looked at him. "We can move into my condo, but you're going to find it a little small."

He smiled at her. "I meant, is the house all right? Do you want to buy something together?"

"I love your house. It's beautiful and big. We can have lots of kids." She grinned. "After we tell my parents, we need to let Hilde know we're engaged."

"And Marisol and the girls, and Shane." He kissed her. "So I was thinking we'd go to Italy for our honeymoon."

"That would be amazing. I'd love that."

His expression turned wary. "Traditionally, the husband pays for the honeymoon. Are you going to be okay with that?"

"Of course."

"Because when I offered to pay for your trip to Italy before, you got really mad at me."

"That was totally different."

He kissed her again. "I'll never understand you."

"I think in about fifty years you'll do just fine."

He grinned at her. "Even if I'm still trying to figure it all out, I know those are going to be the best fifty years of my life."

"Mine, too."

* * * * *

WE HOPE YOU ENJOYED
THIS BOOK FROM

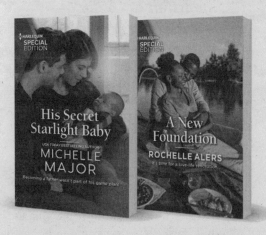

Believe in love. Overcome obstacles. Find happiness.

Relate to finding comfort and strength in the
support of loved ones and enjoy the journey
no matter what life throws your way.

6 NEW BOOKS AVAILABLE EVERY MONTH!

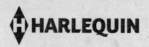

COMING NEXT MONTH FROM

ⒽHARLEQUIN
SPECIAL EDITION

#2839 COWBOY IN DISGUISE
The Fortunes of Texas: The Hotel Fortune • by Allison Leigh
Since she first met him months ago in Rambling Rose at the Hotel Fortune, Arabella Fortune has fantasized about sexy and sweet Jay Cross. Now she sets to find out how he'd intended to finish his last words to her: "I think you should know…"

#2840 THE BABY THAT BINDS THEM
Men of the West • by Stella Bagwell
Prudence Keyes and Luke Crawford agree—their relationship is just a fling, even though they keep crossing paths. But an unplanned pregnancy has them reevaluating what they want, even if their past experiences leave both of them a little too jaded to hope for a happily-ever-after.

#2841 STARTING OVER WITH THE SHERIFF
Rancho Esperanza • by Judy Duarte
When a woman who was falsely convicted of a crime she didn't commit finds herself romantically involved with a single-dad lawman, trust issues abound. Can they put aside their relationship fears and come together to create the family they've both always wanted?

#2842 REDEMPTION ON RIVERS RANCH
Sweet Briar Sweethearts • by Kathy Douglass
Gabriella Tucker needed to start over for herself and her kids, so she returned to Sweet Briar, where she'd spent happy summers. Her childhood friend Carson Rivers is still there. Together can they help each other overcome their painful pasts…and maybe find love on the way?

#2843 WINNING MR. CHARMING
Charming, Texas • by Heatherly Bell
Valerie Villanueva moved from Missouri to Charming, Texas, to take care of her sick grandmother. Working for her first love should be easy because she has every intention of going back to her teaching job at the end of summer. Until one wild contest changes everything…

#2844 IN THE KEY OF FAMILY
Home to Oak Hollow • by Makenna Lee
A homestay in Oak Hollow is Alexandra Roth's final excursion before settling in to her big-city career. Officer Luke Walker, her not-so-welcoming host, isn't sure about the "crunchy" music therapist. Yet his recently orphaned nephew with autism instantly grooves to the beat of Alex's drum. Together, this trio really strikes a chord. But is love enough to keep Alex from returning to her solo act?

YOU CAN FIND MORE INFORMATION ON UPCOMING HARLEQUIN TITLES, FREE EXCERPTS AND MORE AT HARLEQUIN.COM.

HSECNM052

I think you'd better kiss me," she murmured, and her heeks turned rosy.

"Yeah?" His voice dropped also.

"If you don't, then I'll know this is just a dream."

"And if I do?"

She moistened her lips. "Then I'll know this is just a ream."

He smiled slightly. He brushed the silky end of her onytail against her cheek and leaned closer. "Dream, Bella," he whispered, and slowly pressed his lips to hers.

He felt her quick inhale and his own quick rush. Tasted he brightness of lemonade, the sweetness of strawberry.

He slid his fingers from her ponytail to the back of he neck and urged her closer.

Her fingers splayed against his chest. She murmured something against his lips. He barely heard. His head wa full of sound. Full of pulse beats and bells.

She murmured again. This time not against his lips.

He frowned, feeling entirely thwarted. "What?"

She pulled back yet another inch. Her fingertips pushed instead of urged closer. "Do you want to answer that?"

It made sense then. His cell phone was ringing.

Don't miss
Cowboy in Disguise *by Allison Leigh,*
available June 2021 wherever
Harlequin Special Edition books and ebooks are sold.

Harlequin.com

Get 4 FREE REWARDS!

We'll send you 2 FREE Books plus 2 FREE Mystery Gifts.

Harlequin Special Edition books relate to finding comfort and strength in the support of loved ones and enjoying the journey no matter what life throws your way.

FREE
Value Over
$20

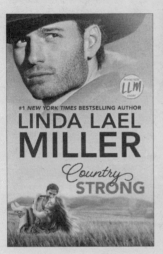
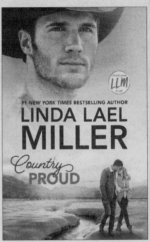